Tony left secondary modern school at 16 and started working in the local F W Woolworth store where he met and subsequently married his wife. Promotion within this organisation had the family moving to different locations, and he eventually ended up at St Ives with his own store management. His four children grew up and attended grammar school, and he was immensely proud of their achievements. When he was asked to move again, it was an easy decision to make, and having settled happily, he left Woolworth and joined Trinity House. The best move he ever made as he really enjoyed the life, and a month on duty and a month at home was sheer bliss. When redundancy happened through the automation of Lighthouses, Tony was devastated but he picked himself up and joined Torbay Hospital as a technician in the sterilisation department, autoclaving surgical instruments. This took him up to retirement age at 65, and he has enjoyed his retirement immensely. Green bowling now occupies most of his time. He still misses the excitement of lighthouses, but that time is now well past.

Dedicated to my four children who encouraged me to publish:
Joanne, Andrew, Mark and Samantha.

Tony Beddard

LAST KEEPER'S LIGHTHOUSE STORIES

AUSTIN MACAULEY PUBLISHERS™

LONDON · CAMBRIDGE · NEW YORK · SHARJAH

A CIP catalogue record for this title is available from the British Library.

ISBN 9781788782319 (Paperback)
ISBN 9781788782326 (Hardback)
ISBN 9781788782333 (E-Book)

www.austinmacauley.com

First Published (2018)
Austin Macauley Publishers Ltd
25 Canada Square
Canary Wharf
London
E14 5LQ

Thanks to Trinity House for images used.

Tower Hill

"Come and join us." I was told by a colleague friend of mine. "It's a grand way of life." As he was an old-school mate, I listened to what he told me of the Lighthouse service, as he was previously a keeper, he certainly knew what he was talking about. My first question was, of course, "Why did you leave if it was such a good number?"

"Marital problems, the wife couldn't manage whilst I was away at sea for my month's duty periods." He certainly painted a rosy picture and I was so impressed. I, next day, wrote off to Trinity House asking for an interview into the service.

By return of post, I was told to make my way up to London's Tower Hill to discuss why I desired to become a keeper within the service. A travel warrant was enclosed for the following day.

Having told the wife of my intentions, it was suggested perhaps the two boys might like a trip up to London as they were on holiday from school. Why not and as I was returning the same day, it should present no problems. Excitement all around.

Arrival at Paddington Rail Station and an underground tube to Tower Hill brought us right in the centre opposite the Houses of Parliament. HMS Belfast in full splendour was anchored on the Thames and was open to visitors. That should more than keep the boys happy whilst I had my interview. I arranged that when they finished the tour of the ship we meet again at the appointed café (McDonald's) their choice.

The magnificent building dominates that side of the river and I entered the big double doors and was greeted at the reception. The list was consulted to check my business and a

9

secretary was summoned to take me to the offices upstairs. The wide expanse of carpet up the central staircase was impressive with large oil paintings of sea battles everywhere. Chandeliers and gleaming brass handrails were sure to impress, the boardroom was entered after a polite knock by the secretary, and we were greeted by a captain in full uniform. A brief word of welcome and I was shuffled off to an office with his Private Secretary.

Such splendour and super efficiency, you couldn't but wonder what was next. The interview went like clockwork. Dictation with signal pad whilst the secretary read out a report was followed by a question and answer session. What had I done since leaving school and was I now free to join the Lighthouse service. Everything was going very well and I was pleased to hear the secretary say to her boss over the telephone that yes, he would do nicely.

Well pleased with the outcome, I had passed the interview and instead of travelling back to Penzance. Would I be so good as to meet the superintendent at west Cowes on the Isle of Wight. You have a return ticket to Penzance, so get off at Southampton and catch the red funnel service across to Cowes. Your first appointment will be stationed at St Catherine's on the Isle of Wight. Your full uniform will be supplied at the depot at West Cowes, and the superintendent is anxious to meet you.

I left Tower Hill on a high and a coffee and burger was most welcome. What to do about the boys, obviously, I needed to telephone home with the glad tidings and could the wife please collect the boys from the station as I was already appointed to go to St Catherine's. Time of train arrival at Penzance was discussed and although pleased about the job, were the boys going to be OK. They travel with me all the way to Southampton and I will make sure the guard keeps an eye.

I waved the train off and a taxi took me to the ferry terminal. My ticket was purchased to Cowes and I was told to hurry up as I might just about catch the hovercraft as it was scheduled to leave shortly.

I ran down the gangway just as the hovercraft was casting off, the boatman ushered me into an empty seat and we were away. I had never been to the Isle of Wight; in fact, I had never been on a hovercraft either. Exciting stuff, the journey to Cowes was choppy and bumpy but certainly fast. On reaching East Cowes, I thought that I better stay aboard as my destination is West Cowes. A short hop over the other side of the river. Cast off the ropes and off we set again. I am sure West Cowes should have been just a little distance to travel and my inquiry to the boatman had him in fits of laughter. I should have got off and crossed over on the chain bridge if I wanted West Cowes.

We returned all the way back to Southampton, the scenery was beautiful but my fuddled brain was quietly cursing. Time was getting on. The ticket office on hearing my tale of woe handed me another ticket which was for the ferry, but unfortunately, the next and last crossing was in another hour and a half's time. Double dam and blast. There was no additional cost the ticket operator smirked, thank goodness, as funds were now getting very low.

When I arrived at West Cowes, of course the depot was closed, the whole staff and the superintendent had long departed for home. The watchman said that I was expected earlier but never mind. "You can sleep in the staff tea room and see the superintendent in the morning." A pillow and some blankets were found and I just thought better get on with it I suppose. A meal and a quick walk around the sleepy town I thought might help, but true to form, everything was closed. A pub was the only refuge and after a pasty and a couple of pints, I returned to the depot tearoom. The staffroom couch was hard as nails and my sleep was fitful. The night watchman was not overly helpful but in the circumstances, I was mucking up his normal routine. He did bring me a mug of tea in the morning and told me to get a move on, as the staff would be arriving shortly. A quick tidy up but of course I had no toiletry gear, never mind, smile and be happy. The staff eyed me with amusement and I was summoned in to see the superintendent as soon as he arrived. The superintendent greeted me and was most obliging, he genuinely understood the quickness of my appointment but the services need for keepers were his main concern. I was fitted up with a uniform from the stores and a taxi was fetched to transport me straight away to St Catherine's Lighthouse.

The Principal Keeper greeted me with open arms and the accommodation seemed to be in good order. "Where are your bags and food boxes?" he asked. I related the story about being appointed straight from the interview and there is no luggage as I thought I was going home that same day.

"Well you had better go up to the shop and get some grub to tide yourself over. When you come back, we can go through the rudiments of your watch keeping routine. You can take the 2000hrs–2400hrs and full training will follow tomorrow." A bicycle up to the top of the hill with a large knapsack was loaned and the local shop did have everything I required but the cost was horrendous, another cheque.

This introduction to the lighthouse service was an eye opener and I have enjoyed the time spent travelling around the country, but a down side for the first two years was not knowing, how long at a station and any time at home. Month off and month away swept away any misgivings when I was finally appointed to the Eddystone.

What a pity that redundancy finished off the keepers. I so miss the way of life but technology it seems can manage without us, and the proof is that the lights are still shining.

A Page of Jokes

A drunken man at a party was well past his best, I am sure he must have started drinking before he arrived. He was a real pain and was shunned by most of the other party guests. He spied a woman across the crowded room and made a beeline towards her, He embraced her clumsily, she, of course, had never seen the man before and promptly slapped his face. "How dare he?"

"I'm so sorry," said the startled man, "but I thought you were my good-looking wife."

"Huh," said the women, "as if I would ever be married to such a clumsy, ugly, drunken disgusting bore like you."

"Good heavens," said the drunk whilst rubbing his face, "you even talk just like her."

"Tony," said her indoors," where is that chicken I asked you to heat up."

"Well," said l, "I did as you asked and heat it up; I did as you said, I have eaten it up, all of it and very nice it was too."

"A hearing aid, what a wonderful modern day invention," my mother said to me one day as she turned up the volume on the television. "Dust proof, waterproof, shockproof, antimagnetic, you can even hit it with a hammer and it remains unbreakable. Such a shame that I still can't hear."

"Why's that?" I asked.

"Well, I can't find it anywhere, it's got lost."

Two flies playing football in the saucer, one said to the other, "You will have to buck up and play better than that as we are playing in the cup next week."

A Cornish baker tried to economise by making the holes in his ring doughnuts bigger, but he soon realised and gave it up as a bad job, as he found he had to use a lot more dough going around the edges.

I do so like a good party where they play jockeys knock. "What's jockeys knock?" I hear you say.
"Well, it's much the same as postman's knock but with twice as much horseplay."

I am not saying I am mean, but when I turn up my toes and croak it, all the money I am owed I have decided to leave to you.

"Waiter, what's this in my soup?"
"It's bean soup sir," he said.
"I did not ask for the history of the soup but what is in it," I asked again.

I think as it's near Christmas, I will buy something special for her in doors. A new Jaguar was favourite, as it had already bitten her twice perhaps next time it might eat her.

CONSTRUCTIVE CRITICISM is a few thousand words of closely reasoned adulation.

A sign outside of the local hospital did read ('guard dogs operating here'). It do make you wonder sometimes, don't it?

There only two types of losers, the good ones, and the ones who can't act.

NOEL. A special Christmas card for someone who has just passed the driving test.

It's most unfortunate that I can't quite make up my mind. No doubt about it but wives usually outlive their husbands. A conversation was overheard one day with the wife saying to her friend that she will be going around the world on a cruise with the insurance money when I die. I think something's not quite right here, why is there no insurance policy for the wife's demise. I must be a bit slow, me thinks.

Alcoholic Keeper

A young friend and working colleague of mine who was most recently made redundant from the Lighthouse service was found to have fallen on hard times. Having split up from his wife and family, he had drunk his way through all his redundancy money in double quick time. I did feel that, perhaps he should have taken more care and kept off the booze, but who can say without knowing the full circumstances of what happened, what's right or what's wrong.

After all the money was gone through drink, he had ended up at the offices of the Department of Social Security, there they listened to his tales of woe and after much deliberation, he was awarded a grant. The grant was awarded to allow him to purchase furniture for his rented council flat. I did think he was extremely lucky that the council could find him a place especially with the long waiting list of the more deserving. The grant was for three hundred pounds. The cheque was cashed at the local Post Office and he was told that full receipts for everything purchased were required by the Social Security officer.

What more deserving case you might ask? As the conditions in the council flat were deplorable. He was using the floor as his bed and shabby curtains were the bedclothes. What the grant was spent on, needless to say, was more booze, bottles of vodka to be exact.

As a fellow keeper watching all this appalling waste, I was most upset to think that it hadn't improved his wellbeing in anyway at all. I couldn't afford luxuries like alcohol, taxed to the hilt like most people. There always seemed to be other things that needed urgent payment and the end of the month usually meant nothing being left over.

"How can a whole grant of £300 be spent on vodka instead of furniture and fittings?" I asked. It was pointed out to me that as 90% of the cost of the vodka is tax, the departmental loss at the Social Security was only £30 on a grant of £300 and the revenue was recovered back into government coffers almost immediately. The grant is only paid once and the poor unfortunate keeper was still drinking and living a life of squalor, nobody to blame but himself. What is his tipple these days, whatever he can get his hands I believe, meth's I expect. What a sad state of affairs. The lesson for all of course is 'EVERYTHING IN MODERATION'.

Battle of the Flowers

How I managed to get myself in such a pickle, I just don't know. I was stationed at Penlee Point Fog Signal Station, which is the Cornwall side of the Tamar. It was a quiet period and I was halfway through a three-week duty. A telephone call changed all that when I was asked to make my way to Alderney in the Channel Islands. *Super*, I thought, *somewhere different for a change,* but it did start a calamitous chain of events best forgotten.

The Superintendent telephoned to say that I was to pack my gear right away as Alderney were working shorthanded and my presence was needed immediately. "As soon as you can get there."

How soon can you get there, no contest, I was on my way. The daily flight from Plymouth Airport leaves at 1800hrs and a telephone booking confirmed my seat to Jersey and a connecting flight on to Alderney that same day. A taxi had me at Plymouth Airport from Stonehouse after using the ferry at Cremyll in plenty of time complete with all my baggage. I did think that perhaps, it might have been better not to have stocked up with grub and goodies the day before but no knowing about my sudden move to Alderney, I didn't intend to leave it all behind. The packing was crammed into two large holdalls, and a backpack, my uniform I could wear which would save packing space.

The weather was looking grim, as fog seemed to have rolled in for blanket coverage of the airport, not uncommon at Plymouth apparently. A delay on leaving was inevitable but hopefully, it might clear and we could complete the flight at some time later this same day. I waited and the coffee shop was doing good business. Nearly two hours later, we lifted off and made the trip to Jersey.

Jersey Airport was bathed in glorious sun even at the lateness of the day. I had missed the connecting flight to Alderney because of being late from Plymouth, so there was nothing for me to do but get a bed and breakfast hotel for the night. The airport at Jersey is relatively small and miles out from St Helier with sparse accommodation anywhere in sight. A taxi was summoned and my baggage was piled into the boot and it dropped me off in the town centre. The taxi fare was paid which took nearly all my cash and I thought that perhaps I should have got some further funds when I had the chance.

Hotels in the centre of St Helier are numerous and struggling with my baggage towards the nearest was my first thought and get out of that rain; also my arms were beginning to feel the strain. The reception desk girl looked on in amazement at my request for a bed for the night as she asked didn't I know it was Battle of the flowers week and the whole town was brim full. "You will be lucky to find anywhere," she said. She did try telephoning to several on my behalf but all to no avail. Everywhere was full. I did say a broom cupboard would do, but no, nothing sorry.

I tried more hotels and guesthouses but the answer was the same, nothing. Soaked, tired and very little money left, I wondered what to do next. Perhaps if I smashed a window so that the police would lock me up for the night at least I would be out of the rain and in the dry. Silly reasoning and I thought the sensible solution was to return to the airport and wait in comfort for my next morning flight. I telephone for a taxi using the last of my cash and returned to the airport. A cheque covered the fare and what coinage I had left was the tip.

I struggled around to the airport's main entrance and found that the double doors were locked; it was closed for the night. A loud rap on the doors brought the security guard to see what was happening and his Alsatian dog kicked off letting me know that I was not welcome. After gesturing and saying that the airport was closed, he did finally unlock the doors and I was invited in out of the rain. The whole sorry tale of my misfortunes was told and bless him, he said I could wait in the lounge area till my flight in the morning. My sodden uniform and bedraggled state was I think the deciding factor.

The doors were locked again and I settled down on to the seating and thanked the nice man profusely. He even found a blanket and pillow but he warned that the cleaners had to be cleaning all night around me. I settled down and rested my aching arms, and curled into the blanket to sleep. I was awoken in next to no time by a cleaner with a cup of tea, I did thank her but I would sooner have preferred to sleep.

Early next morning, as the airport came alive and the cleaners had departed apparently. The smell of coffee and cooked bacon from the catering area wafted across to where I sat, but with no money left, I would just have to go without, I am not using any more cheques. The flight to Alderney was scheduled for 0930hrs. My ticket covered the flight because of the fog yesterday and I was escorted to the aircraft by the pilot. I was a little surprised at his attire, A Biggles type of headgear, a handlebar moustache and a brown Leather Flying Jacket. What was a little bit bizarre being that he was carrying a wooden orange box.

The aircraft to say should have been in a museum is unkind, but when each wire strut was twanged to make sure it was still functioning properly, I found it most disconcerting. The orange box I found was for passengers to use as a step up into their seat as each seat had its own door. Four passengers besides myself and the Pilot. We took off beautifully to a clear, cloudless sky and landed on grass at Alderney Airport. We trouped into the small wooden hut and everybody's luggage and bags soon arrived on a buggy.

Another taxi was used to get to Alderney Lighthouse and yet another of my cheques, the last one in the book. The Principal Keeper greeted me and bid me welcome, I was just glad to have finally reached my destination.

Wonderful location, fabulous Island and I spent five weeks enjoying cycling around discovering all that the Island had to offer.

Bert's Eggs

The MS 'Oldenburg' arrived at Lundy Island after yet another difficult crossing from Bideford.

The tide tables showed that full floodwater over the Bideford sandbar would mean an early morning sailing time. Very few passengers in the month of January make the trip, but essential supplies for the island population had reached an alarming low state, the 'Marisco' tavern was down to its last few barrels of beer. Immediate remedial action had to be taken, as the island without any beer was unthinkable.

If the wind was in the wrong direction and the landing beach under the South Lighthouse was taking its usual pounding, the sailing was often cancelled as this meant nothing could come ashore safely. There is only the one safe unloading bay. It was always touch and go in the winter months anyway, and unfavourable weather conditions ensured the island would have to wait for precious supplies when this happened. That day, it was decided that the sailing could proceed as the wind was in the right quarter. Soon the much-needed stores were off loaded and transported by tractor and trailer up the only island road to the top of the cliffs. The precious mail sack was taken to the Lundy office for sorting. It was customary for the off-duty lighthouse keeper to make the long trek up to the top of the island to collect the mail and whilst there, perhaps partake of a few bevies. Bert, the South Light Principal Keeper, would make an early start and be up there in readiness for the mail after collecting a few items from the shop. The departure of the MS Oldenburg after completing her unloading usually took about four hours from first dropping her anchor.

This always signalled that the 'Marisco' Tavern would soon close, as any visitors had to return to the ship for passage back to Bideford.

Bert had partaken of a few pints but as the bar was to be closed, extra pints were drawn to see him through the afternoon. Sometime later, when all his beer had been drunken, Bert thought it best to make his way back to the lighthouse. He did wonder what he should have for his tea and fool that he was, he realised perhaps he should have done the shop when it was open, too late now, but something would present itself. One step forward and one step back, Bert progressed along the dusty road and was making good progress. When the farm was in view, it brought an idea into Bert's fuddled mind; fresh farm eggs will make a nice teatime treat. The door to the chicken coop was soon opened and the hens had done a fine job; Bert filled his bag.

Eventually, Bert was back in the safety of the lighthouse again and as the eggs had taken the rough trip home showing several broken and cracked, it was decided to have them scrambled. The cooking was well under way when there was a loud knock on the door which was most unusual as the climb up the cliff was enough to deter most people. John, the farmer, was admitted and offered a cup of tea. "Well what you got cooking, Bert?" was asked.

"Me tea," he replied, "I purchased some eggs from the shop earlier."

"Well that's funny said John, I do believe you have been pinching my eggs from the chicken coop."

"Not me," he said, "these was bought."

"Next time you pinch my eggs do remember not to leave the mail in the coop."

The red-faced Bert was speechless and John turned the screw for all he was worth every time they were in the pub together. Several pints had to be paid for to appease John. It must be said that Bert's scrambled egg tea did eventually cost a small fortune and John supped very well for months.

Bishop Rock

The Bishop Rock Lighthouse stands sentinel at the approaches to the Isles of Scilly. The 167ft tower must withstand the full force of the Atlantic swell coming across from America. The first tower was completed in 1849, but was swept away completely the following year. A second tower was once again built but was found to have extensive damage to the structure. A new tower had again to be built encasing the whole tower and elevating the height by another 40ft. The Bishop Rock Lighthouse is now really two towers, one encasing the other. Such is the might of the enormous waves it must withstand from the Atlantic swell; it is a testament to the skill of the building.

I was stationed on the Bishop Rock when I was informed that a Professor from Newcastle University would be coming out on the next relief to test the towers worrying cracks at the base of the structure. Bishop Rock relief would be done first from Sennen Cove to allow maximum time for him to do his checks. The helicopter would return after completing the Seven Stones, Longships and Wolf Rock, and Round Island crews turn around, giving a good four hours before he would be lifted off again.

The helicopter landed and the Professor was brought down through the hatchway. As the helicopter took off, I could see that he was most concerned about the speed of its departure. His small briefcase and box of tools was lowered to the gallery and we entered the lighthouse. Radio and signal work followed to say that the professor was on board.

He was hopping about in some discomfort as he said he desperately wanted the toilet, he had drunk so many coffees and teas whilst waiting at Sennen Cove that he would be grateful if we could show him where the toilet was. A toilet is a luxury on some towers but on this Lighthouse, it's bucket and chuck it. Blue chemical sit on, with plenty of catchment water at the ready in buckets.

Down two levels and out of the bedroom window, he was told. Off he went to relieve himself. As I went down towards the kitchen level, I came across the Professor trying to climb into the window opening. "What are you doing?" I shouted.

"Having a pee," he said.

"Button up and get yourself down before you fall out into the sea. Do your business in the bailer pan and throw that into the sea, with the wind mind. It's a good job the bailer pan is attached with a good chain otherwise that would have disappeared into the sea." His face was a picture and realisation suddenly dawned. I left him to it and carried on down to the kitchen.

The window recess is made of gunmetal, because of the thickness of the tower, there is enough room between the outside window shuttering and the inner but to climb into this space is foolhardy and reckless, the fall into the sea onto the rocks some 150ft below would be fatal.

When he returned to the safety of the kitchen, I asked, "What were you thinking?" And he admitted that he had misunderstood, he was so desperate and he did think it a bit unusual, but needs must.

"Sit yourself down," I said, "and tell me what you want to achieve whilst here on the Lighthouse." He wanted to go on the very base of the tower to check for fissures and cracks and take samples of the granite stonework. Well given his antics at the bedroom window, I had better not let him out of my sight.

The sea, though sloppy, was not too bad to allow access to the setoff, but I explained that he could go down with myself as long as he did exactly what was asked. A lifejacket must be worn and a safety harness attached to a rope held by a colleague from the doorway. A radio was slung around my neck and the other keeper also had the second radio. The heavy, steel doors were opened and the climb down to the set off by the dog steps was only about 30ft but the Professor was looking most anxiously at the setoff, the narrow ledge didn't look very wide. I went first and made sure that his rope was taut and as a further safeguard, another rope tied us together. A lengthy decent to the set off where I showed him the chain hand holds. "Do not leave hold of the chain," I said. "If you get swept into the sea, you will probably take me with you, and pulling you back could be difficult." His tool bag was lowered and attached to the bottom brass dog step. He was eager to start and his crab like moving around the tower to inspect various parts was comical. We were, of course, in the lee of the incoming waves and wind but as soon as you edged around a certain point, white water and spray let you know that you had gone far enough. The professor's glasses were covered in salt spray in no time and I indicated that we should return into the tower.

This close to the elements I could see that it was not safe. He didn't want to comply and pulled like fury to get around that little bit further. I grabbed hold of the chain either side of his body and pushed him against the tower block wall. "No," I shouted into his ear, "it's not safe so please do as I ask." He reluctantly crab walked back to the dog steps again. I told my colleague by radio to keep a tight hold of the rope as he climbed back up into the towers safety. He was disappointed I could see but you can't mess about with the sea conditions as they were. It's a long way from Newcastle but safety always comes first. He was content after stripping off the lifejacket to explore the rest of the tower. His little hammer was hard at work on most of the levels and measuring strips could be seen everywhere.

The time was fast approaching when he would have to put the flying safety suit back on but he still wanted to carry on with his inspection. The radio announced the helicopter would be here to pick up the Professor in 15 minutes. "Next time," I told him, "perhaps you might like to choose the summer weather and stay on board the lighthouse a little longer so that you can complete your work."

He was lifted off the Bishop Rock and returned to the mainland and we never did find out what the findings of his work revealed. But the nutty professor from Newcastle did write and thank everybody for the kind assistance and help he received. The trouble with landlubbers is they don't understand the power of the sea.

Cards and Scrabble

Being captive on a lighthouse for a month at a time, games play an important part of filling in the spare hours. Scrabble is favourite but card games can be played with only two keepers, whilst the third keeper is sleeping his off duty watch period. Serious consideration in playing to win at all cost unfortunately means sometimes that the true spirit of fairness goes out of the window. Playing in an aggressive manner is not to be encouraged; being competitive should be everybody's aim but in striving to be the best always remember to play fair. The whole month's matches are recorded and a chart to see who comes out on top is the normal way it's done.

Rules of Engagement

The decision of who goes first is decided by choosing a letter out of the shake bag. The player nearest to the letter 'A' is first to start and the next player in clockwise order after that.

Picking your seven letters from the shake bag should be done in strict order of play having already established who follows who, of course this should be done without looking into the bag, any deviation from this rule will be met with disapproval from your fellow keeper players and could result with a sharp slap upon the wrist. A vote by the remaining participants will ascertain if the player is allowed to continue.

Placing your letters upon the playing board in the assembled order of play will only score if the opposition players don't consider a challenge is necessary. If two challenges are successful in a row, then the player will miss his turn gracefully and throwing a tantrum is to be avoided.

Sportsmanship at all times is paramount and encouragement in producing long words should be applauded.

Brother keepers who score consistently well with clever play should be congratulated with a pat on the back and it is in everybody's interest to further high quality play. Upon completion, however, a well done and a handshake of congratulation is the normal but do be aware of spiteful crushers. If any one player continually wins and shows off, then frustration amongst his fellow keepers could result in foreign bodies being put in his nightly beverage, so be aware.

Time spent pondering must be cut to a satisfactory level, a player who is considered taking far too long to make his play will be asked to speed up or miss his turn. We all realise brain power is sometimes lacking in some keepers but slow play is much against the true spirit of the game and minds will wander as stimulation is lost.

Finally, anyone who throws the board complete with the playing tiles upon the floor, will obviously not be asked to play again as this practice is very naughty and very bad sportsmanship.

Casquets Lighthouse

The Casquets Lighthouse lies about midway out in the shipping lanes between England and France. The relief by boat is notoriously rough because of the high fall and rise of the tides. Dangerous rocks around the Channel Island group have accounted for many lives lost with shipwrecks. Casquets, Les Hanois, La Corbière, Sark and Aldeney make up the Channel Island group. I was lucky enough to have been posted to most of these Lighthouses at one time but the odd one out is La Corbière which is operated by the French Service and not Trinity House.

Casquets Lighthouse was reached by helicopter from Guernsey and collecting my store of food for the month was achieved mostly in the superb market at St Peter Port. All the butchers and fruit stalls are in rows competing against one another for your trade. The fish market is typically French with the cooking of crab and lobsters amongst the fresh fish, wonderful. The locals are mostly friendly but the local dialect (Patois) leaves you wondering what is being said.

The relief the next day was without incident and on landing, I was surprised to see that my gear and food stores were being loaded onto a train. A monorail from the base of the quay ran up the steep incline to the Lighthouse towering above. What a smart idea, but riding aboard was not permitted. The steep pathway alongside the rail I could walk and unload everything when I reached the top. Before the rail was installed, a horse pulled everything up on a cart and was stabled on the Island. I should have thought the horse was more work than was benefited.

The Island was a dream posting, twin towers, bedrooms with enough space to swing a dozen cats.

The routine was soon established and the fog signal was quiet for most of my stay. The Principal Keeper was a man who lived on Sark and was a wonderful cook; his gastronomic skills were a pleasure.

A lobster pot was part of the daily chores. Clambering over the rocks on the morning watch to see what you had caught was the highlight of the day. The first time the Principal Keeper took me down to pull the pot was an eye opener. Discovering two large crabs and a lobster, I thought we were in heaven. Rebaiting the pot and throwing it back into the right chosen sandy bottom off the edge of the rock was a skill and the giant of a man with strong powerful arms had long ago mastered the Technique. The Principal Keeper gave me a crab to carry back to the dwelling and said, "If you hold it by the back legs, the claws can't reach your fingers." I gingerly tried this method as we set off and instantly dropped the crab and it tumbled back into the sea. The Principal Keeper was not amused. The legs tweaking my hand I thought it was the claws. Oh dear, he shook his head and I was only entrusted to carry the ropes instead of precious crabs. "Remind me to bring a bag next time," he said.

Most morning watches produced bounty from the sea, but when you surfaced from slumber at breakfast time, you had to be careful where you put your feet as the mornings catch were scuttling around the flag stone kitchen floor. It was customary for the afternoon watch to cook the shellfish and present the picked-out crabmeat for tea. One time, a large dogfish had got entrapped in the pot and the culinary skill of the Principal Keeper produced a superb meal from this catch. The trick is skinning the fish. Hooking up on a spike and ripping the skin down the flesh needs strength and a good heavy pair of gloves. The finished meal looked like shredded wheat but the taste was excellent.

My understanding that dogfish were fit for nothing and were returned to sea had me thinking perhaps I had a lot to learn.

The huge flag stoned courtyard on the Casquets Lighthouse is enormous, more like a parade ground and I hadn't realised the significance of this until it rained. The rain tipped down and it was all hands turn to and scrub the courtyard clean, as this could then be used for catchment water. The tanks were near empty at this time so it was essential to be quick. Seagull and bird droppings were the main problem, so get scrubbing. There was an unnoticed tilt to the paving pushing the water to a clearing tank; the bung in this tank would only be removed when the water was clear. A glass was constantly checked to see that no foreign bodies were floating. When satisfied, the water fell into a second tank and the same process was again used to inspect the quality. The Principal Keeper would only allow clean, clear water to join our precious using tank. What happened, of course, most of the time was that the rain stopped before we had finished scrubbing. Wait for the next deluge, I suppose. It did get to the stage where I dreaded the rain and the weather reports took on a new meaning.

Because of the location of the lighthouse which was right in the migratory path of migrating birds, a job I found I disliked was to pick up the dead bodies around the lantern gallery. In the night, the birds would fly into the beam of light and pitch headlong into the glass. I was told to pitch them over the side and into the sea, if they were alive, they could fly; if not, it was a quick and certain death. I did think that perhaps some could be saved and a large owl with wing damage I hid in the workshop wrapped in cotton wool and a saucer of milk. I checked daily its progress but it succumbed to the inevitable in the end. My two colleagues who had seen it all before sympathised but said it's just nature's way. Great big softy that I am, I still did try to rescue some birds and I like to think one or two survived through my efforts.

Casquets had suffered in the war years as keepers were apparently killed and the tall-tale signs could still be seen in the tower roof where bullet holes after German fighter planes had used the tower for target practise. The surrounding rocks still produced empty shell spent cases.

My time on Casquets was all too short before I was once more returned home via Guernsey to Plymouth. The customs at Plymouth Airport because of the uniform was a real bonus as my duty-free cigarette tobacco allowance was often exceeded as I was waved straight through. The Channel Island group I looked forward to each posting but unfortunately, I never did get the chance to return to such a wonderful Island.

Casualty Evacuation from a Rock Tower

The Neil Robertson stretcher was never designed for use in such confined spaces as a lighthouse. This was made abundantly clear when the Principle Keeper slipped on the engine room floor whilst mopping up a spillage of oil. He had broken his ankle. Seventeen stone of quivering flesh strapped into a prone position on this apparatus didn't seem to restrict his vocal cords as choice language still gushed forth between his yelps of pain and curses. A radio call for assistance was made and, apparently, a helicopter would be dispatched to air to lift him ashore within the hour.

A painkiller of pethidine could perhaps have been administered if only we had been on the first aid course, but typically, the only trained person on board the lighthouse was the Principal Keeper (Sod's law). If the two keepers, although super fit, ever manage to lift such a heavy load up to the top of the tower and on to the helipad, I would be very surprised, in fact it would be a miracle.

Who suggested using a pulley I can't say, but it did seem a clever idea at the time. The Principal Keeper on hearing this suggestion, however, was not so sure and wanted a boat ashore. The helicopter was on its way he was told, so let's get on and rig the pulley.

The pulley wheel was hung from the top of the tower from the helipad, the length of rope was passed through with just enough to reach the set off down below, where the still cursing Principal Keeper watched in rising trepidation. A section of safety netting was removed to allow the stretcher to pass through onto the helipad without interruption. He then could be air lifted off to hospital for treatment, that was the plan.

Now that everything was ready, both keepers took the strain and pulled very slowly with hardly a jerk on the line so as not to cause any further unnecessary pain. It was such a strain even though both keepers managed to keep the upward climb of the stretcher continuing to the top of the tower; it was not without its terrible strain on the arm muscles. Gradually, it reached the top and both keepers heaved a sigh of relief as our aching muscles were screaming in protest at the work load. What a heavy strain. The rope was secured around a stanchion post and our arms could at long last be rested. Sam, my colleague, raced off to see to the hanging stretcher with the shouting Principal Keeper at the top of the tower. He was supposed to pull the stretcher through the netting and when he said that he had hold, I released the rope from around the stanchion post. Unfortunately, a seventeen-stone burden was just too much and I held on grimly to try and stop the stretcher's fall, I found myself hanging on for dear life as I started to go up and the stretcher started to come down.

The stretcher and I met about halfway and the handle gave me an almighty smack in my groin, which knocked the stuffing out of me and made my eyes water, but I held grimly on. I continued to the top of the tower until my fingers became trapped in the pulley wheel and luckily, the stretcher had hit bottom, the Principal Keeper was all right apparently, he had landed on his bottom. Sam's grinning face now only three feet from my own suggested that maybe all yet might be put right. Sam suddenly disappeared, the silly boy, and was next seen at the base of the tower attending to the Principal Keeper's needs. I was left hanging on for dear life. The Principal Keeper I could see was all right through my tear-filled eyes as he started to undo the restraining straps. A groggy step on his ankle soon reminded him that this act of folly was perhaps most unwise and he fell over and landed away from the stretcher apparatus onto his backside. The first thing he noticed was the stretcher now freed of its load had started to move upwards again, his look of astonishment alerted Sam and his desperate jump couldn't prevent the stretcher continuing its upward journey and Sam unfortunately landed on the Principal Keeper's broken ankle and both were sent sprawling.

As my fingers were now freed from the pulley wheel, I started to fall downwards. I held on tight to the rope and started the long trip down. Yet again, I met the stretcher about halfway on its journey up, it scored another hefty blow but this time to my ribs. I still held on grimly and continued my way towards the base, mercifully about four feet from the setoff and the inevitable crunch the rope in the pulley wheel jumped and stuck fast, the whiplash effect of this was to catapult me into Sam's foolhardy attempt to break my fall. At this point, we were all rather slow to consider the now forgotten stretcher, which with no restraining weight began once again to fall towards the setoff. At the bottom of the tower, it bounced catching me a further blow upon my shoulder and back before sliding into the sea. *Good riddance*, we all thought.

All together, the three keepers were in a very sorry state and the sound of the approaching helicopter landing on the pad brought much needed strength to put things right. The Principal Keeper was eventually winched off to the helicopter and then off to hospital. Still cursing and shouting, it will be nice for some peace and quiet now he's gone.

Sam and I now working shorthanded eased our aching limbs, cuts and bruises and the station watch keeping continued for the remainder of the duty period. What was apparent after this calamitous exercise is that if a fellow keeper is unfortunate to injure himself, wait for skilled assistance and take the training course for first aid.

David's Broken Arm

The engine room on the Needles Lighthouse is to say the very least, cramped. The three engines dominate the whole of what little floor space that there is. The switch gear board hasn't altered since it was introduced when the Lighthouse was electrified from paraffin lamps many moons ago. Giant buzz bars for each separate engine and dials with equalising turn wheels for voltage control. The scene could be in keeping with a Frankenstein movie set but in reality, it works a treat when you have mastered how to manipulate the controls.

A twin forked buzz bar is engaged when you have got the engine running and putting the lever into the two receiver brackets usually is the forewarning of flying sparks everywhere. The first time this happens is a bit alarming, but remembering to keep your hands well away and your feet on the rubber mat means the electrical current is contained. Direct current 100 voltage and not 240 as in all appliances ashore. Alternating current is what most people are familiar with but everything on the Needles its 100volts. Converters do come into play for certain things like radiotelephones and the television, but the normal from the engines is direct current. The control of the current has to be adjusted up or down depending on which engine you are using to achieve the proper voltage. A safety guard rail at waste height keeps your body well away from the apparatus, you take liberties at your peril.

What happened on this fateful day was that David had said a small stone had lodged in his work boot; he was trying to get the offending item out whilst precariously balanced upon one leg and leaning on the mains switchboard safety bar. Both hands being occupied, one holding on and the other in the process of shaking his leg to dislodge the troublesome stone, I suppose it looked to John the other keeper as he entered the engine room that David was receiving an electric shock. This of course was completely the wrong conclusion reached but understandable in the circumstances I suppose. John shouted a warning above the noise of the engines and sprang into action; he picked up the heavy wooden starting handle and swung a mighty blow down upon David's arm, breaking contact with the power fuse board as he thought. The arm you could tell at a glance was broken from the peculiar angle that it was bent backwards away from David's body. His scream could be heard even above the sound of the engines.

Later whilst awaiting the arrival of the helicopter to whisk David ashore for treatment at the local hospital, John was asked the simple question 'why' did you do it, why did you strike such a fearsome blow upon David's arm. "Well, the first lesson in first aid for electrical shock is never touch the casualty for fear of you also getting a shock; DC (direct current) tends to take hold of you unlike AC (alternating current) which throws you off. Needles Lighthouse is of course DC and I didn't want what I thought David was getting."

David did say when he eventually returned to work some months later that in all fairness, the extra time spent at home was almost worth the broken arm. But my suggestion of giving him another whack upon his other arm was met with instant refusal. "No thanks, once is more than enough."

Don't Bite Your Nails

Andrew was a pleasant enough child. Intelligent to a degree so his first schoolteacher said but his one failing was that he would bite his nails. His mother threatened him, punished him but was quite unable to cure his habit of biting his nails no matter how she tried. Then one day on the verge of despair, she discovered that Andrew had a morbid fear of becoming fat (like his dad), whereupon she told the boy that the one infallible method of becoming fat was to bite your nails.

This declaration to the child seemed to work like a charm for a while, but it did produce an interesting sequel on the very next week. What happened whilst visiting the local supermarket to do the shopping with his mother, Andrew happened to notice some very large pregnant young women being served in front of the queue. He sidled over to the young women and seemed to be intrigued with her bulge. Fascinated, he stood and stared at her until the now highly embarrassed women eventually said, "What is the matter my young friend, do you know me?"

"No," said Andrew, "I don't know you but I do know what you have been doing. Biting your nails perhaps?"

Journal Entry

The Trinity House vessel after a strenuous day of lifting buoys and replacing chains dropped anchor and the crew were given the option of a night ashore. The coxswain and several of the crew took full advantage of this and when finally returned to the ship to sign in were much the worst for wear. Inebriated (drunk in fact). The coxswain was in a very sorry state, if he wasn't drunk, he was a very good actor, but whatever his very drunken state, it was noted in the journal.

Coxswain drunk on his return from shore. The following morning saw the coxswain up before the captain, and he was forced to admit that his drunkenness was a correct entry, but was it really necessary. The captain was adamant that the entry was factual and was going to stay in the journal. The coxswain then asked if it was, therefore, all right to enter any such remarks when next he had the watch as long as they were absolutely true, the captain was a little taken aback but reluctantly agreed.

The captain had to go ashore the following day on business and checking the journal entry the next morning, he was astounded to see that what had been written by the watch keeper, it was noted in the journal (today the captain returned sober).

Fire Fighting

Fire on lighthouses is a thing which fills me with dread. An isolated rock tower miles from land with storage tanks filled with fuel for the generating engines is something which you take seriously. To escape the fire, you would have to take to the sea. Rough seas or the fire, one you drown, the other you burn. Lighthouses by the very nature of their construction are like chimneys. Storage tanks at the base and if a fire took hold, the air would funnel the flames upwards through the rest of the building. Electrics like radio beacons and wireless telephones need aerials and although these are used to send signals, they can also act in reverse as conductors for lightning. An expanse of sea when lightning is about likes nothing better that to latch onto a way to earth itself. An incident whilst on watch on Round Island Lighthouse showed the destructive power as a lightning strike blew the radio beacon apparatus off the wall. I was doing the weather reports and was in close proximity when it happened and my hair stood on end, I was very lucky. This shows from out of the blue, lightning can strike at any time.

Firefighting courses are essential. The week's course all the way up at Norwich was coupled with a First Aid course and a chance to meet fellow keepers doing the same thing. A real expense paid knees up in the evenings and good accommodation. But the work at the airport location and maritime college had to be done first.

The first day was spent in the classroom mostly showing the different fire extinguishers. How they work, how to use them and what to use them on. Fire is governed by three basic principles, heat, fuel, air, take away any one of the three and you extinguish the fire. A red triangle symbolises this principle. Remove one side of the triangle, and you have cracked it. Foam extinguishers, water extinguishers and CO_2 extinguishers use the wrong one and you could soon find yourself in trouble. And this was fully brought to light on the very next day.

The Airfield at Norwich was attended by the twelve keepers who were asked to don their boiler suits in readiness for the training. The instructors were straight down to business. A gruff parade ground Sergeant major type of fellow soon instilled order, so that the work could begin.

The first was a fat fire (chip pan) take away the air by covering the top with a cloth, each keeper had a go. It did show that to take the cover off the fire, it soon reignited. Turn off the heat or remove the pan, do wear the gloves provided.

The second was a burning pit filled with oil and thick black smoke, and when fully alight, this had to be attacked with a fire hose. This was a three-man job and it was explained that you must control the fire with a procedure of advancing using a fine mist from the hose to take away the heat. The lead man on the hose was chosen because of his bulk in size. I was number two and well sheltered from the tremendous heat. I do think that the fire was winning and as we got nearer, the heat and smoke was awesome. The lead man was coughing and spluttering and obviously, he had taken the full brunt, he let go of the hose and scarpered, I found myself in the front and it was now a different story. Sweeping backward and forward with the spray as instructed, we eventually mastered the beast and it was extinguished. Covered with grime and soaking wet, we were cheered back into the rest of the group. The instructor was shaking his head and the poor unfortunate lead man was given a right ear bashing. I stood tall as praise was heaped upon us for continuing the exercise. Each group had to do the burning pit routine and the bulky fellow had to do it all over again. Twice in fact.

The next was the burning oil in the enclosed area. A 6x6 tray fully alight in the confined space had to be put out. Why I was chosen was, I suspect, because I was so smug about the hose business, the instructor decided I needed a reality check. He tossed a big red extinguisher at me and told me to put out the fire; it did look as if it was getting out of hand. "Hurry up," he said. I went forward, pressed the handle and a jet of water hit the fire which exploded. Whoosh, flames everywhere. I picked myself up and I am sure the hair singeing smell was me. The instructor asked, "What happened there then, the fire is still going."

"I attacked the fire as instructed with the extinguisher that you gave me."

"Oh dear, did you check what sort of extinguisher it was."

"Well you gave it to me," I said.

"There's the lesson, always make sure you use the correct type of extinguisher, never use water on oil in that way, you saw what can happen."

The next was a smoke-filled room using breathing apparatus, goggles, hard hats and crawling through lengths of piping runs, very tight course and the cylinder on your back kept catching with the low headroom unless you crawled on your belly. When this was completed, we were walked over to an aircraft hangar and told this was being filled with smoke and we couldn't yet enter. When it was ready, we could find our way out again. We could see obstacles, the tables and chairs, a settee, a set of ladders, bags of who knows what. All these things we could see and remember where they were before the closing of the hanger doors. Should be a doddle. Two teams split evenly were asked to escape as quickly as possible. A stopwatch would record the times.

The naughty instructors had purposely let us see where everything was before closing the doors and then promptly moved everything around. On entering the hangar, you couldn't see a hand in front of your face. Extra walls seemed to have been put in, as keeping to one side just didn't work. It was simply ages going around in circles and getting nowhere, until eventually, a door handle was found so we could escape. The instructor was smiling and thought that perhaps we now realised the importance of breathing apparatus and how it could save lives.

What an excellent job, there were showers at the facility as we badly needed a good scrub and the boiler suits did save our clothes to a certain extent but the smoke smell remained for the rest of the week.

Let's get on to the first aid, at least the nurse will be a bit more understanding and not have a sadistic streak hopefully. Firefighting although a trial at the time, it did stick in the mind just like it was supposed to do, learn the basics the hard way I suppose.

Fishing

Fishing on Lighthouses is not only recreational but a useful source of supplementing your food choices. I do like fish anyway and you can't get fresher than catching it yourself. Depending on which Lighthouse you are stationed, the way to fish must be varied to suit the circumstances. The Wolf Rock is deep sea and a hand line drifting out on the tide with a lure I found most productive. Yet the Eddystone Lighthouse, because of the reef encircling the tower, is very difficult. You have to get your line over the reef and then on bringing back the chances are high of being snagged on the weed and rocks and losing all your gear. Kite fishing is the answer. From the gallery at the top of the tower, get your kite in the air with a long strong line and a trail of catgut weighted line with a float, this can be baited or you can use a lure. How deep you want to fish must be worked out beforehand and the trace cut under the float decides at what depth. The wind direction is irrelevant as miles from land means once over the reef, it's safe fishing. A steady wind keeping the kite still with little movement is the trick and practise and patience will get you your reward.

What sort of fish is usually in the lap of the gods, surface fishing with a float or deeper with bait. Mackerel, Coalfish, Pollock, or if lucky, a nice bass. The Eddystone reef is renowned as the breeding ground for bass. Fishing with a rod is next to useless and I have found a strong hand line gives the best results.

Fishing from the Wolf Rock gallery using a hand line with a lure, an afternoon's work would normally bring 30–40 fish, mostly Pollock. After an hour of filleting and bagging ready for the freezer, it's fresh fish whenever you want it. My favourite was fish pie. Halfway through the duty months period is favourite as the Paraffin freezers are half empty, no room at the start.

Ingredients for a fish pie, fish, hard-boiled eggs, white sauce, cheese sauce in my case and mashed potatoes, a handful of prawns if you have any, cheese topping and you don't have to be stingy with the fish.

Bringing the fish to the top of the Lighthouse gallery has its problems, when the line is taught, you know a fish is on the line, a quick jerk to make sure it's well and truly hooked and then a long haul to the gallery. When the fish leaves the sea, it's a straight pull up the 150ft tower. Many a good catch has been lost on its way up, but patience and perseverance is the name of the game. A red food box is always ready to catch the still thrashing fish, otherwise it's over the side again and back into the sea.

My freezer box on going ashore was always full of fish fillets and family and friends were most appreciative. How much has it cost depends on how much I must spend on lost lures and gear but well worth the effort, I am sure and it keeps me out of mischief and well fed.

Friends of Beachy Head

I was appointed to Beachy Head Lighthouse just in time for a Christmas duty period, away again for Christmas. I was instructed to meet my keeper colleague at the address where the boat relief was to be done at Newhaven. The day before relief was needed to collect my food stores and pack in readiness for the boat out to the Lighthouse. The Royal Sovereign was to be done by the same boat and the keepers were doing much the same in gathering together their own food and stores.

The weather did not look favourable and if the seas didn't calm down, it was suggested that the Beachy Head relief might have to walk from the Gap under the high cliffs from Eastbourne. This had been done on many occasions but timing had to be perfect with the keepers coming ashore as we started from the Gap. The Royal Sovereign, being a tower platform out at sea, would have to wait for calmer waters. Christmas was a mere eight days away and my purchased food packed and ready had to be left with the boatman, he promised he would deliver as soon as the weather would permit. Carrying so much gear across the lengthy walk to the lighthouse proper meant I could only take a few bits and pieces. Milk, bread, butter, coffee, tea and a pack of sausages. Everything else would be delivered.

The walk along the beach was started and a radio message to the Lighthouse telling them about our progress was made so we should meet about halfway was soon done. The keepers could only get off the Lighthouse when the tide permitted, usually trousers were rolled up and shoes and socks were in a backpack and put back on when on solid ground. When we met them at halfway point, there was no time other than to wish them well for Christmas and hurry forward to the Lighthouse.

We arrived at Beachy Head with the tide already lapping at the rock base. Taking off our own footwear and socks and hitching up our trousers, we jumped from one sunken drum of concrete to the next to gain access to the set off. Without the drums of concrete, we would have been trapped between the 300ft cliffs and the incoming tide, no chance of returning to the gap before the tide cut us off. That's why timing was essential. A pleasant enough tower but I do so hope the rest of my food stores arrive as one pack of sausages aren't going to last.

A daily request to the boatman asking when he could make a safe trip to us with the rest of the gear was met with little response for an immediate answer to the lengthening problems of grub shortages. I borrowed tins and food from the store cupboards of the resident crew but it was most worrying that the packed meat and vegetables would spoil before it ever arrived. After six days, I was really getting worried on short rations, but the friends of Beachy Head arrived by the dozen to save the day, apparently an annual event. The other keepers knew about what usually happens each year, but I was kept in the dark. No wonder they were so free and easy with my food requests. They had worked out the tides and started early to be at the lighthouse with all manner of goodies. Collections in the local pubs and clubs to look after those keepers aboard the lighthouse at Christmas. When everything was aboard, they departed back to the gap so as not to be cut off by the incoming tide.

You name it and it was there; I have never seen so much stuff. There were bottles of wine, turkey and all the trimmings. Christmas pudding, Mince pies, smoked salmon, cheeses and enough beer to float a whole ship's crew. Bottles of whiskey, a bottle of rum a bottle of gin, they had even remembered the tonic water and mixers. The Principal Keeper was he said tee total, "What a shame my other colleague and I will just have to see what inroads we can make on our own." A great Christmas was had and when eventually the boat landed my own purchased goodies, it was a struggle to polish everything off before I was due ashore. What a lifesaver.

Funny Cornish Maid

Seen on a barmaid's chest who was from Hayle,
Were tattooed all the latest prices of the ale,
But on her behind, for the sake of the blind,
Was the same information but in braille?

Fuse Tester Operational Instructions

It has been brought to my attention that there are some Keepers who unfortunately are being very wasteful by throwing away perfectly good fuses for no other reason than not know how to use the testing equipment. To remedy this problem, a list of operational instructions has been put together for circulation to all manned working lighthouse stations. Even the slower witted keepers amongst our personnel should be able to grasp the rudiments as long as the rules are followed.

The following instructions for testing all fuses must be adhered to and the laid down procedure as in these notes of how to achieve a satisfactory conclusion will easily be mastered.

Rule 1. Make sure that the correct clothing is worn, rubber soled shoes or wellington boots eye goggles and protective gloves. It is also, perhaps, a clever idea to make use of the rubber apron.

Rule 2. Always make sure that the left hand is in your trouser pocket so that contact with earthing is avoided, if left handed of course, then the right hand should be in your pocket.

Rule 3. Placing the fuse across the brass terminals with the light indicator lamp will only work if the power source is healthy, have you checked the condition of this supply?

Rule 4. Indicator lamp fails to light after checking the supply source, this means the fuse is duff or it could of course be that the operator is not fully complying as in the instructions.

Rule 5. If the fuse is tested and found in a satisfactory condition but the indicator lamp bulb fails to show the normal reaction, then the lamp should be taken from this appliance and tested in another complicated piece of circuitry called a bulb tester.

Rule 6. Having now decided that the correct power source, bulb, shoes, goggles apron gloves and hand in pocket, you are ready to proceed.

Rule 7. If the indicator lamp shows by glowing that particular fuse is in fact healthy, it means that you have completed this difficult procedure, if on the other hand the indicator lamp fails to show a flicker of response, it's back to Rule 1 and start again. It could be that the fuse is not functioning correctly but can you be sure. Do not throw away valuable fuses only to find it's the operational incompetence of the person using this system.

Rule 8. If at this stage, you are still not sure, do call another member of the staff who will give guidance and training so that in future, he is not called upon to give assistance in such a mundane undertaking.

Rule 9. There is always, if still not sure, the possibility of telephoning, the works depot and speaking to a qualified electrician who will give you the benefit of his superior knowledge, do be careful mind as problem solving is not always in the best interest of the service.

Rule 10. Under no circumstances should a screwdriver be used. Don't be a bright spark.

Rule 11. If the fuse tester can't be mastered, then a good tip is to use a six-inch nail, this can be cut to the appropriate length and should cure all problems. Do stand well back if using the nail system, just be very sure of what's best.

It's Always Dullest Before the Yawn

There are some very strange people about and in most walks of life, Lighthouses have more than its fair share. On all the lighthouses I have been on, time plays such an important part of your everyday existence. How you fill in the long watch periods can decide if the job of being a lighthouse keeper comes easy, or is a constant struggle. Myself I have found that I am well content with a delightful book or a fishing line. Games of cards or a game of chess and my favourite of course is scrabble. The time seems to fly by and a monthly turn of duty is over before you can blink.

One keeper I was serving with had a most unusual habit of using quotations all day long, every other phrase or saying was either a proverb or a famous quote, but he would always get the thing wrong. Whether this was by design or an accident, I was never quite sure, some of his utterances were very entertaining and I found myself also catching the quotation bug, much to the annoyance of the Principal Keeper, who thought we were both off our rockers. Many an hour devising new and interesting mixes of proverbs and metaphors just to outdo each other was the normal; it became a real trial but a constant source of amusement. It was purgatory for the Principal Keeper mind, but perhaps that was why it prospered and grew. The brand of humour to most people was lost and we found that our feeble efforts and permutations had them shaking their heads thinking we were gone quite mad, but we thought an active mind kept us on our toes. A knowing wink between us both would be the shore tale sign that we had scored a hit and if nothing else, we did learn our proverbs and quotations.

The list is endless and the variations could change to suit the daily circumstances. Although my quoting friend has long since passed to pastures new, unfortunately, I have still retained the now familiar habit of constantly quoting proverbs but always in the new amended form, much to the annoyance of family and friends. I do get more of my fair share of funny looks and pitying side-glances, but they, that know me, have long accepted my weird humour.

It's always dullest before the yawn	(DAWN)
A fool and his money are always invited out	(SOON PARTED)
A bird in the bush is worth two in the hand	(HAND, BUSH)
Ask no questions and you will get no answers	(TOLD NO LIES)
Cold hands no hot water bottle	(WARM HEART)
Time and tide wait for Trinity	(NO MAN)

That's it, the list could go on and on but give it a go yourself, you might just find your own creative skills will produce some gems.

Jailbird

Confessions in the wee small hours is a habitual trait in the lighthouse keeping game, you get to hear all sorts of stories and keepers tell you the most unusual tales. I had a fellow keeper (Paul) who was an excellent work colleague and an all-round pleasure to work with; his one failing was perhaps he would whistle whilst going about his normal duties. The saying goes amongst sea faring folk is that there is no whistling whilst at sea, 'whistle up the wind' at your peril.

Paul decided he would open up one day after braving another heavy storm in the dog watch he confided to me that he had spent a considerable time in and out of prisons and remand centres prior to joining Trinity House. The offences had ranged from burglary to breaking and entering; the drug habit had to be paid for.

"Why did you embark upon such a silly road?" I asked and was told it was, I expect, sheer greed and laziness, an effortless way to get money to feed his drug taking.

"You want these things and you can't be bothered to work for them, so you steal them, whatever you can get your hands on instead." I was appalled and quite surprised, as since I had known him, I thought butter wouldn't melt in his mouth, such a nice man. He did point out that he was now well out of that downward spiral and the error of his stupidity was well past. I was intrigued and asked, "Why did you start on drugs in the first place. Was it an unhappy childhood then or a lack of parental love and attention?"

"No, nothing like that; it was just mixing with the wrong people and thinking I was clever."

My look of astonishment was I suppose why he continued to unburden his thoughts, and he said that he did have several jobs over a considerable lengthy period but they didn't last long all those early mornings were such a strain. "What with being out burgling all night, I couldn't manage to get up in the mornings, so the jobs had to go. Since I have been working for Trinity House, mind I have kept well out of trouble, no mischief at all. Being stuck out on a Lighthouse is just like being in jail, you are miles from anywhere and if I think about it though, perhaps I might have been better off inside, as at least in prison you got your meals cooked for you and your laundry was washed. No now that I have seen the error of the stupid drug scene, mixing with the other inmates was very hard and my family felt the problems I had caused as much as myself."

"Well, I never," I said. "Here's me doing my best in life and paying my way but I get to do bird every time I come out to this rock tower lighthouse anyway, stuck on the Wolf, Bishop Rock, Longships, Eddystone I suppose it's much the same." Thinking about what had been said I soon realised that no comparison could be made between the two, I was lucky doing a job I liked and a month's break meant six months off a year, you can keep your prison I am well content. Choice is a wonderful thing and holding your head held high beats stupidity.

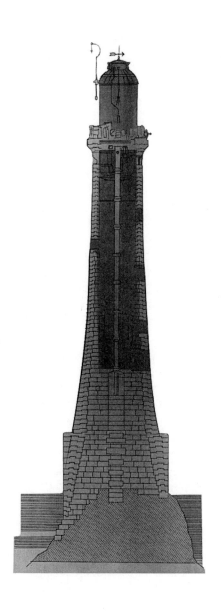

Just in Time

The Needles Lighthouse is a safeguard to shipping making its way up the Solent to Portsmouth and Southampton. It is built at the end of a line of chalk cliffs giving the Lighthouse its name. A storehouse carved out of the cliff stores all the fuel tanks that are needed for the running of the diesel engines. The tower flashing white beam light on top of the 109ft is supplemented by fixed sector lights of red and green to warn of dangerous rocks. When ships are on passage if they can see a red light, it means they need to change their position until the green sector light is shown. The high and low tides are a constant problem as sand banks come into play. Rounding the Needles in any sort of craft without care or guidance can end in disaster.

Rough weather in winter is a constant reminder of the limitations of boat reliefs. December and Christmas at home would be a real pleasure this year as I seemed to have done more than my fair share in past Christmases. The relief date for my turn ashore was fixed for the 18th December. The weather did not look good and Tony, the boatman, based at Yarmouth forever the optimist said, "Don't worry, just wait and see." The 18th arrived and I could see that there was no chance of a changeover of crew. 19th, 20th, 21st and still the seas were pounding the setoff landing. I had already done an extra four days and it looked as if I might even be spending Christmas as well. My constant packing of my bedding and having to remake my bunk each day was frustrating. Tony, the boatman, promised to take a look at the possibility of doing the relief on the 22nd but the weather was just too rough and fog made its appearance to add to the problems. The 23rd was also tried and the boat was watching for a chance to come alongside but all to no avail.

Christmas Eve and I was still marooned and if anything, the seas were getting even more lumpy. I don't know, but it sure looks as if I am stuck here. Who contacted the coastguard about the overdue but I suspect it was the boatman, bless him.

The big Sikorsky coastguard helicopter from Lee on Solent have agreed to affect the crew change over as it's Christmas. Our helipad will not be big enough or strong enough to take this massive helicopter but perhaps a winch cable can drop and lift us off. Keep an eye and radio contact for further details.

True to form, the helicopter arrived and my opposite number was lowered onto our helipad along with his baggage. The cargo nets received his boxes and my own bags were lifted into the body of the helicopter. The cable and harness were next lowered so that I could at last get off. About 6ft off the helipad, the helicopter started to move crablike away from the helipad and over the sea, instead of just being above the pad, I was above a long drop of about 150ft and dangling on the end of the cable. The helicopter had decided to circle around the Needles and put me down on the top of the 400ft cliffs. It was later explained that the helicopter could only hover for so long in one position.

I was dumped along with my gear and baggage to be met by Tony and his van. The radio work from Tony thanked them for their kind assistance as they sped away back to Lee on Solent again. The Yarmouth ferry and the railway got me home for Christmas. That was a close call and I feel the close working relationship with Tony and the coastguard had more than a little bit to do with my relief being done at all. I was truly thankful and wrote and thanked all concerned but dangling below the helicopter is not for the faint hearted and I don't fancy doing this exercise more than once, whatever the circumstances.

Lighthouse Keepers Now Gone

The lighthouse service is still struggling gamely on,
The lights are now dimmer and the Keepers are gone,
Fog signals are not wanted and nor are rock lights,
It's now a different service, it's lowered its sights.

It was always a pleasure to watch the ships in the night,
The strength of the beam it was such a wonderful sight,
Ships so they do tell me, don't need keepers no more,
I suppose this is so true, but I cannot be so very sure,

You get what you pay for or so that's what they do say,
So, a second-class service, lights have had their last day,
Computers and technology have now taken over control,
I suppose it's the way forward but it's still a huge blow.

Well me old matey, it's I suppose now redundancy for me,
The prospects are not very rosy; I'll think you'll all now
agree,
The cost cutters have done it, they have pruned to the bone,
I only hope that the shipping can get safely back to home.

Liming the Landing

The Wolf Rock Lighthouse is situated 20 miles out at sea between Land's End and the Scilly Isles.

A main feature of the Wolf Rock tower is a substantial landing stage adjoining the tower; this was used to great effect when the lighthouse was constructed. The granite blocks were landed on this platform by boat, and the dovetailed stone was cemented into place whilst the lighthouse was built over a period of some five years. The sea and currents around the Wolf Rock are not for the inexperienced seaman, as being swept overboard from the setoff platform would mean very little chance of getting back to safety again.

The high tides and waves constantly washing over the setoff means that seaweed growth is a dangerous hazard and has to be treated as often as the keepers can get down onto the platform.

Scrubbing chloride of lime into the seaweed is the only way to combat the weed gaining a foothold.

The landing must be cleared constantly so that when stores or water and diesel fuel are landed from the Trinity House Vessels, it can be done with relative safety. Chloride of lime is lethal stuff and should be used with the utmost care; my own clothing will testify just how it eats into whatever material it comes into contact with. Two keepers dressed in wet weather gear, wellington boots, facemasks and goggles scrub the chloride of lime into the weed before the tide once again covers the setoff. The dry powder is mixed with seawater but no matter how careful, it gets everywhere. The third keeper from the safety of the tower doorway watches the sea and can shout a warning if the waves present a safety hazard. Large container ships or tankers passing miles away create a wash which can piggyback upon a wave and hit you when you are not looking, being swept off the platform is not a wise option. The watching keeper will shout and the scrubbers will run to the day mark obelisk with the buckets and brooms till the water has subsided.

The lifejackets although an encumbrance is necessary as if you are dumped into the oggin, the chances are slim of getting back aboard but at least you stay afloat. Chloride of lime eats into the seaweed in double quick time and when the tide once again covers the setoff, you can see how good a job has been done when on the next low water tide. If you have not completed the task properly, then it's down again to finish what you have missed.

Washing the yellow wet gear in seawater when you have finished is essential as the lime will eat the stitching, and leggings and jackets will fall apart. The lime plays such devastation upon the small creatures that live in the weed. Sea lice, sand hoppers and small crabs hate the stuff and even the limpets close up shop to make an impenetrable seal against the lime and press themselves on the rocks even tighter. But the lime clears everything back to the granite rock surface, the barnacles and limpets are gone as is the weed.

When the job is done, it's nice to get back into the tower to wash and drink a welcome mug of tea and clear your dry painful throat as the lime has penetrated up your nostrils and although it clears your head, it's most unpleasant. The weather especially in the winter months usually means no liming can be done, but the weed soon takes hold again and the only hope is that the other crew cops for liming. The blue metal containers showing the dangerous chloride carries a warning for its usage but I feel sure the damage has already been done, like the small sea creatures I feel the best thing is to stay well clear.

Me, Blood and Needles

Why some people shy away from needles or faint at the mere sight of blood I just don't know, but it seems I am one of those people so afflicted. I can lift heavy weights, fight a lion if called upon but the sight of blood, especially my own leaves me totally useless. I can skin a rabbit, butcher a lamb carcass but the harder I try to fight this fear, the worse it gets. I will just have to accept that I am just a big jessie when it comes to blood and needles. Unfortunately, I have been caught out on numerous occasions.

What happened on this fateful day was an appointment had been made whilst on my off-duty period from the lighthouse at the doctor's surgery with the nurse for a long overdue check-up. The early morning time was agreed and when I marched in, the practise was in full swing with patients filling most of the available seating. The surgery was packed. Appointments were apparently running late again.

My appointment time came and passed and it was obvious that waiting would just have to take its course. My turn eventually arrived near an hour late but would I like to see the nurse in room two, adjacent to the waiting room. Most patients had appointments with the doctor which was well away from the waiting room in the rear of the building. The nurse was bristling with healthy vigour and keen to get on as quickly as possible to help clear the backlog of patients. Without any preliminaries, she proceeded to pull up my shirt sleeve to enable her to take my blood pressure, this was soon achieved and it seems that my heart was pumping like a traction engine, first class no problems. Next item on the list was to take a sample of blood, I did mention to the nurse that I didn't much like the sight of needles or blood, she laughed and said, "What a big strong fellow like you, don't be silly, but if it makes you queasy, don't look whilst I take the sample." The needle with the bulbous glass middle section lay on the desk in front of me, my eyes seemed to be riveted to the dish and no matter how hard I tried swivelling my head away to focus on something else, it constantly returned to the loathsome needle. The search for cotton wool swabs seemed to be taking ages and of course, it was then that the telephone rang. Why Mrs Taylor's water sample had been contaminated couldn't be explained but the telephone conversation was taking a very long time and all this was adding to my discomfort as my eyes were glued to the needle in the dish before me. Was the room getting unbearably hot and my body spasms and dry throat didn't further help the situation. My left leg had developed an uncontrollable shake. "Do take hold of yourself," I muttered to myself, "and for goodness sake, hurry up nurse."

I was fighting back sheer nausea but putting on a brave face. The nurse at long last finished the telephone conversation and Mrs Tylor was asked to bring in another sample. The nurse was all bustle and purpose again after the interruption. She remembered to remind me to look away and a sharp prick soon had me gritting my teeth, after what seemed an age the nurse said, "There, that wasn't so bad, was it? You can look now," as she showed me the bulbous middle section containing my blood. Oh dear, why was it suddenly so very hot. I do remember putting my hand out to stave off the edge of the desk as I fell but that's all. I awoke with my head being bathed with a wet cloth and the nurse was making soothing noises as she wafted smelling salts under my nose. I was fully stretched out on the floor but what was more alarming was that the whole waiting room was rubber necking to see what the commotion in room two was. The receptionist was swinging the door to cause a draft across my prone body which I felt was most unnecessary. Sheer embarrassment made me spring up rather too quickly and my obviously still shaky legs were not quite ready. I pitched forward taking the arc lamp and the weighing scales sailing across the carpet showering glass towards the waiting room. The rush of patients scattered and the nurse in a high-pitched voice told me to sit down and stop still before and more damage is done.

"Enough is enough and shut that blasted door," she shouted to the receptionist. I do think, perhaps, the nurse was feeling the strain. After a reviving glass of water which I sipped as instructed, the nurse started clearing up the shambles I had caused. Whilst writing up my notes at the desk, I did notice that a blue star was affixed to my file. I did ask what the significance of this was and was told to make sure that whoever attends to me, please stress that they always read the notes first.

What a carry on, and even now some years later, people still point me out to those who were not there and retell the story and chuckle at my misfortune. I do tell they that ask, it's in the blood I suppose. One consolation is that I am never asked to attend hospitals very often. They do say medically that over virile males are the main cause of this fear of the sight of blood and I think perhaps this could be spot on, there has got to be a good reason why a healthy strong fellow like myself should be so afflicted.

Misuse of Station Equipment

My attention has been drawn to the fact that station equipment at lighthouses is often used in all sorts of ways that it was never intended or designed for. This serious problem is more widespread than Trinity House could possibly comprehend. I do know that it's beyond most Keepers' understanding how this is allowed to continue but perhaps the few who blatantly misuse equipment in this way, might like to reconsider their actions. The mentality of just a few is jeopardising the safe use of equipment in the proper use for which it was intended or needed.

The ingenuity perhaps might be congratulated but I am sure Trinity House will think differently and wonder why it was allowed in the first place. Keepers' feelings on this delicate matter are noted but please stick to the rules and don't indulge in this misuse of equipment no matter how you might feel it's justified.

A following list highlights some of the items involved:-

Loud Hailer	1. Used instead of the radio to tell yachts to bog off if straying close to rocks.
	2. When bad language is used, but please not on the airwaves.
Water pump grease	Cure for bunions
Lavatory brush	Back scrubber, don't mix them up
Engine Starting Handle	Crab claw cracker and hard nuts.
Rocket Sticks	Whittling wood when bored
Station rulebook	Wobbly leg support.

Ear defenders	Worn especially when work is mentioned
Ship to ship radio	Ear wigging on frequencies
Battery rubber apron	Used when gutting fish
Fog signal	1. Used to attract keepers on the beach.
	2. Retaliatory ear bashing for noisy workmen on station.
	3. Keeps duty watchman awake through the night.
MPX OIL	Sun cream.
PGO DIESEL	Barbeque fuel but can leave a nasty after taste.
Heavy ropes	Spliced together for hammocks hung from helipad.
Flag locker	Bunting at parties and knees ups.
Heaving lines	Kite fishing string
Methylated spirit	Replaces gin, quite intoxicating
Rubber matting	Cut into lengths to save blood and guts on clothing when fishing

The list is endless but Keepers do know right from wrong and these misuses must stop afore someone gets hurt. Principal Keepers do take control and stamp it out, it's naughty.

Nab Tower

The Nab Tower guarding the Western entrance to the Solent is one of the strangest lighthouses that I have served on. I was appointed to this Station for a month's duty period and told to liaise with the pilot boat cutter at Southampton who would transport me out to the Nab. I collected my stores and food for the month and was ferried out with the Principal Keeper in the launch. My colleague did look a bit under the weather as I think his consumption the night before of so many sherbets had left him with an almighty hangover. His thick, broad, Scottish accent was very difficult to comprehend first time around and I was forever asking him to repeat what he had said. Quick fire utterances left me none the wiser half the time and in drink, it was an impossibility to understand. His toothy smile I feel meant that he had come across many others in exactly the same boat.

The first sight of the Nab tower was not what I expected; it was like a giant gasometer with a permanent tilt to one side. The lean was alarming; it looked as if it would turn right over in a gale.

The fact that it was built during the First World War was testament I suppose to its stability. Painted black, it was an imposing sight. A set of iron ladders down to a sea level platform was the only entrance to this fortress. The pilot launch steadied alongside this platform and watched the waves, and when the skipper was satisfied that a landing could proceed, we were told to jump across the gap where willing hands could pull us onto the platform. I did worry for the safety of my colleague, but he was sure footed and landed safe. A safety rope was hauled into place for the baggage. It must have been one of the quickest reliefs ever.

The launch sped off as soon as the other two keepers had got aboard the launch and pleasantries were exchanged before a wave of farewell. The labyrinth of passages and tunnels to the living quarters were most confusing and in my month's duty, I never did quite manage to fathom out which way was quickest. The tilt of the tower was even more pronounced when inside, everywhere you walked was uphill or downhill. The circular structure when I tried to work it out meant that if you started in one place, you would eventually get back to where you started again.

My small bedroom was against the engine room bulkhead and the constant thump of the diesel engines kept me awake most of the time and if the fog engine in unison with the generator engine were both in use, it was purgatory. The large bell above my bedroom clanging to the already constant noise was a further hazard. After a week of very little sleep, I was like a zombie but eventually tiredness took over and I was able to block the noise out.

Two navigation lights on the roof of the tower were covered in the daytime so that when lighting up time was needed, you had to remove the coverings. One evening when I went to do the covers, a plague of flying ants had descended on to the Nab tower; I suppose the fact that it was painted black had something to do with it. Peeling off the covers to exhibit the lights, I was soon covered completely with the swarm, not very nice. The obvious choice was to take a shower afterwards but the little blighters had even clogged up the water system. You wouldn't believe the pesky varmints could cause so much havoc. It took us days to get everything back to normal.

Because of where we were placed in the Solent, yachts were racing in different races all the time and the yachting committee constantly asked the keepers to take the sail numbers as they passed. Cowes, Yarmouth, Portsmouth, Southampton, all with hundreds of sailing yachts were constantly out racing. Different classes, large 'K' class yachts and (Edward Heath) in his Morning Cloud sailed around us. He did wave. The rougher the weather, the more the sailing fraternity seemed to enjoy the racing but the rain and wind whilst stood taking sail numbers didn't inspire my middle of the night vigilance.

The tower was usually a turnaround marker and tacking around and racing each other made for some calamitous incidents. The tower was often hit with the tightness of their turns.

I suppose the Christmas hamper as a thank you from the organisers did in some way make the discomfort of spending hours watching the antics of the yachtsmen seem worthwhile.

The Principal Keeper lived in Cawsand which is just in Cornwall. The Plymouth-Torpoint, ferry across the Tamer river, takes you around to Cawsand and Kingsand overlooking Plymouth from the quiet sleepy villages. It's a beautiful unspoilt part of the world.

When we had finished our month's duty period, we decided to travel home together on the train from Southampton. He got off at Plymouth, and I continued my journey on to Penzance. The canny Scotchman did like a glass or two of the amber nectar (whiskey), a bottle was purchased as soon as we were ashore. He said we could share it on the train, but as he had bought the scotch, I could perhaps supply the coffees. I have never bought so many coffees in all my life and at British Railway prices, I could have bought a couple of bottles of scotch for what I had to spend on coffee. I think I might have had been had. I am convinced that my tipple each time was more of a splash than a full measure.

But that's life.

Needles and the Small Room

Operational instructions were written as a consequence of circumstances that really happened whilst on board at the Needles Lighthouse. To make any sense of these instructions, it would help if I were able to make clear the whole set up at the lighthouse.

Lack of thought and no written instructions were wholly to blame, and the stonemason and myself didn't see the funny side of what happened. Now some time later, of course, we can look back and smile, but at the time, it could have developed into serious consequences. A heavy fist up the throat.

What happened was that on the Needles Lighthouse, the wee small room is situated at the top of the tower, one level down from the service room, the shower is right next door and is sandwiched in between two fridges. In this height of luxury, a proper lavatory bowl is fitted with a proper lockable door. This might seem funny to most people but if you could see some of the facilities on rock towers and lack of privacy, you would also be appreciative. Bucket and chuck it was more often the normal and always remember which way the wind is blowing.

The Needles throne is a real blessing. The outlet pipe running right around the service room and outside of the tower it drops straight down to the set off some 100ft below on the leeward side. The pipe is bent at an angle to continue over the side of the tower towards the skirting which surrounds the lighthouse, this is designed so that the waves are broken up and turned back into the sea. The discharge from the pipe is well clear of the landing and is soon swept away into the sea. Now Clifford, the stonemason, had been sent out from the

Works Department at Penzance Depot to effect repairs to the skirting cobbles as the heavy winter seas had begun to wear away some of the stones, it was in urgent need of strengthening and some considerable pointing. This, of course, could only be achieved in good summer weather with low spring tides so that the maximum time for hardening off, before the tide once again covered the worked area. The tide dictated that early morning first light 0500hrs was best suited and the weather this August morning was just right to reach the lower skirting levels. As I was the morning watchman, I was pressed into being the volunteer to assist Clifford with the mixing and passing of materials. For safety reasons, Clifford couldn't work on his own as he could easily soon get swept away. A safety rope was fastened around the both of our waists and life jackets, although cumbersome, were the order of the day. Work was progressing well and the waves sweeping along the setoff didn't encroach the pointing and the cement hardener was having time to do its work.

At this time of the morning, my two keeper colleagues should have been fast asleep in the confines of the tower but for some unknown reason, one of them decides to visit the wee small room. Now I should point out here that only sit down jobbies necessitates a visit to the small room, lesser bodily functions are achieved without using precious flushing water. The first we know of course that one of the keepers is up and about is the outlet pipe is showering us both with a torrent of water and effluent, we were both covered from head to foot and so surprised that neither of us could move before the flushing sequence had finished. The shouts and choice language I feel sure should have aroused the sleeping keepers but, nothing, nobody appeared. The air was blue and although the worst of the muck was washed away with seawater, we couldn't move fast enough to strip off our work gear and get into the tower for a shower. Stripped down to underpants, we climbed back to the safety of the setoff and climbed the stairs to the bedroom level. The bedroom door was closed and upon opening, it showed both sets of bunk curtains were drawn, so there was no way to tell or decide which of the keepers was to blame. After leaving the bedroom once more to find clean fresh clothing and a good shower, it was decided to tackle and find who was responsible later. I just hope Clifford calms down, as he is a big brute of a man with a temper. A nice cup of tea should do the trick and that's it now the tide has turned so no more working below.

That very same day, I decided to pen the operational instructions notice and to this day, it is still pinned to the back of the door, and many a visiting keeper has had a chuckle but at the time, it wasn't so funny. Clifford and I often laugh at the happenings of that fateful day but it will never happen again as each time I go anywhere near that outlet pipe, the small room is locked and the key is safe in my pocket. A locked door ensures my safety, no good getting older unless you learn life's hard lessons. Once bitten, twice bitten; the general rule should of course be twice shy but I am not taking any chances.

The work was finally finished but lucky for me, the tides and weather dictated someone else did the honours and just as well, Clifford did finally see the funny side, mind it did cost the guilty keeper several beers in the pub when ashore again.

Noddy Noall's Demise

Time has caught up with me and my moving to a new lighthouse station has meant that the Lighthouse news sheet will now have to do without my feeble attempts at witticism as mind provoking comments under the nom-de-plume of Noddy Noall is now at an end.

If the attempts made you think about the Lighthouse service in perhaps a different light or even a less serious attitude, then all my efforts were not in vain. To say what I liked in a jocular way and poke fun at the Lighthouse authority is surely healthy, but controversial comment always seems to upset somebody.

I have enjoyed Lighthouse Keepers' feedback whilst some seemed to appreciate my mischief making and laugh at the stories; there were others that moaned and couldn't see the funny side at all. I have derived a great deal of satisfaction from seeing my efforts stir reactions both good and bad. Loath or love Noddy's own inimitable style, it did fill a gap and provide much needed food for thought within the fledgling magazine news sheet, which was dying for want of input by the keepers. The editor, Gerry, was always pleased with my efforts and encouraged me to write more articles but in the end, the circulation died along with the Keepers.

Noddy is no more, so sleep content those of you who clap their hands in glee at his passing, but for those who mourn Noddy's demise, I truly thank you. The light is now gone extinguished by hurtful criticism. Keep your quills sharp and write in and say what you yourself think, help to the keep the magazine alive or it will not survive. The ever-diminishing small band of Keepers is shrinking fast, what is going on,

where will it all end? Take up the reins and keep beating the drum. Keep the wicks trimmed and see the light.
Noddy is no more.
Yours Posthumously,
Noddy Noall

Obnoxious Keeper

It does take all sorts in life as they say and luckily, in the Lighthouse keeping game. It was my privilege to work alongside some likeminded people 'Harold', I met for the first time prior to the relief at the guest house that was being used by the Keepers on the Barbican in Plymouth. The evening meal completed; it was suggested perhaps a few last beers might be in order as it would be our last chance for a month. A selection of pubs was available and after three different venues were visited, I realised that Harold had an aversion to paying his round. Short arms and long pockets do spring to mind. "Enough of that nonsense, if nothing else, I am a quick learner." What a tight-fisted colleague to be saddled with. The word from other Keepers warning of Harold's antics should have prepared me for what followed but great softie that I am, the benefit of seeing for myself how things work out was uppermost in my mind. An early night then, as I was not going to pay for any more beers and I vowed that it will not happen ever again.

Breakfast the next morning was strained but the spread on offer of cereal, a full breakfast with a pot of tea was first class. Toast and butter with an array of different toppings to complete a good start to the day. Why Harold thought it was appropriate to finish the last of the milk straight from the jug and pocket the individual marmalade and jams I can't fathom, but I was not pleased and told him that he is an embarrassment. The other guests at the adjoining tables shook their heads in disbelief.

The relief from the Barbican quay to the Eddystone was an eye opener, but that's another story.

I did ask Ginger Mutton, our skipper, on the boat relief if Harold's behaviour was the normal way he conducted himself. He just smiled and laughed and said, "It didn't take you long to work it out for yourself, good job I don't have to spend time cooped up with such a miserable excuse for a keeper."

Oh dear, fun times ahead, I thought, *but we will just have to see how the duty period progresses.*

Stuck on a lighthouse with just the three keepers could get on your nerves if you were not able to get along together. You are reliant on each other to make the Lighthouse function in a ship shape fashion. It was my misfortune to be posted to the Eddystone at the time of a notorious Principal Keeper in charge. Harold the oddball from Worthing. He was renowned for being difficult and if he could make the month's duty period a trial, he would go home happy. He doesn't know me very well and I am made of sterner stuff, it should make for interesting times ahead.

My time on the Eddystone was mostly enjoyable, as my fellow keepers knew how to keep on top of what was happening. Harold was a dipper, what is a dipper I hear you ask. It is someone who helps themselves to your grub. You daren't leave anything about as it would shrink in size or disappear completely. I did learn very quickly to store biscuits and cakes well away under lock and key. Coffee, tea bags, tobacco. It was not very nice.

The Principle Keeper didn't smoke or so he said, apart from an occasional cigar. But to leave your tobacco tin about was foolhardy, the dipper never wasted an opportunity. I did tackle him on several occasions about dipping, but a red-faced denial was always his answer. The best way to stop this unsavoury practise was to deny him the opportunity by never leaving your stuff about, sad but a true fact of life.

The watch system was that my morning watch always followed his on the next day. I noticed silly little things, like my pumping up fuel and fresh water, as was the routine, seemed to take ages and I soon realised that Harold wasn't doing any pumping at all. When it was his next morning watch, I set a trap to see if any pumping had been done. The semi-rotary pumps were still in the marked positions showing water and fuel were being left to the next watchman. Very naughty. When I asked if both had been pumped, I was met with an angry denial and my checking each time when he was on watch showed an improvement to this daily task. Washing down the metal stairs each morning was part of the watchman's duties and after finding two broken in half matchsticks under the lowest stair, I realised these were put there to see if I had washed down. I replaced the matches and told my keeper colleague about my discovery and told him that having removed them I put them back with two more of my own on the next flight of stairs. Sure enough at breakfast time, Harold announced that he had caught me out, as I hadn't washed down the stairs. "Well," I said, "are you sure about that?"

"Yes," he said, "the two matches were still in place, which proves it."

"Oh dear, yes, I saw those and replaced them and put some of my own on the next flight but you will find that they are a step up and not where you put them originally." He left the kitchen in a right strop and the door was slammed in his fury.

Both keepers were smokers of roll up tobacco and it was decided as the Principal Keeper didn't smoke, he said, that an ashtray on the table was emptied as soon as the cigarette was finished. He couldn't abide the smell of smoke so he always opened the window and door to clear the air. And the ashtray was usually thrown into the corner. Mike, my colleague, would nudge me as it was now my turn to have a roll up, and the whole open and closing routine would start all over again. A month of these petty squabbles were tiresome but also entertaining and the meanness of the Principal Keeper who couldn't see that he was the loser as everything shared between Mike and myself left him out on a limb. Good job he was one of a kind, how he lasted cooped up for so long without being ditched into the sea is a miracle.

The next relief, I decided not to use the same guesthouse and told the boatman that I would be there at the appointed time and my list of requirements were to be as usual. Ginger's little shop was brilliant and he, bless him, always managed to pack in something extra. The rest I brought from home. The first that I realised that something was amiss was a telephone communication from the Superintendent's office asking why my expense sheet showed overnight allowance for a night in Plymouth as the Principal Keeper had said that I had travelled up to Plymouth on the morning of the relief. Well, I had heard it all now, what a despicable thing to do. I explained that if a rail ticket showing the date of my travel was on the day prior to the relief, would that be acceptable. There is no invoice for a guesthouse as I stopped with my relations who live in Plymouth and they kindly dropped me at the quayside in plenty of appropriate time, which incidentally had been already arranged with the boatman. The reason for not sharing the same guesthouse as the Principal Keeper was that he was an obnoxious man and a total embarrassment at the guest house. Whilst I had the Superintendent's ear, I also informed him of what was happening on the Eddystone and he explained that something was already afoot to remedy the situation. My expenses were quite legitimate and he apologised for having to ask.

The following month saw a new Principal Keeper appointed to the Eddystone Lighthouse and Harold was shifted elsewhere. Nothing was ever explained and the new fellow was such a pleasure to work with that I did wonder if perhaps Harold had shot himself in the foot. Whatever the circumstances, Harold had got his comeuppance.

Ode to Our Young Ken

RETIREMENT COMES ONLY ONCE OR SO THEY DO SAY,
ENJOY IT NOW TROUBLE FREE FOR WHILST YOU MAY,
'COS THOSE YOU LEAVE BEHIND WILL JUST STRUGGLE ON,
LONG AFTER YOU'VE FINISHED LONG AFTER YOU'VE GONE.

YOUNG KEN IT'S AN ERA 40 YEARS AND PLUS MORE,
WE DON'T KNOW HOW YOU STUCK IT WE CAN'T BE SURE,
WE DO KNOW YOUR LEAVING HAS LEFT A LARGE GAP,
I SUPPOSE TRINITY WILL FILL IT, HOW, JUST LIKE THAT.

GOING TO THE HOUSE FOR YOUR SCROLL ON THE HILL,
WITH DEPUTY MASTER, DRINKING TEA OF YOUR FILL,
DON'T BE CRITICAL OF THOSE BREATHERN WHO'S IN POWER,
REMEMBER RIGHT OPPOSITE IS THAT AWFUL BLOODY TOWER.

THEY DON'T MAKE 'EM LIKE YOU, THEY GONE BROKE THE MOULD,
THE OLD SCHOOL IS FINISHED OR THAT'S WHAT I BEEN TOLD,

LIGHTHOUSE KEEPERS ARE ALWAYS A FUNNY OLD BREED,
AND YOU WAS SOMETHING SPECIAL, A GOOD ONE INDEED.

On Ken's retirement from Lundy Lighthouse, I quickly penned this ode for Ken and had it framed in the Island office. The Lundy news, a very limited edition and circulation took up the article and featured it in the next edition. The last day of Ken's duty before he went ashore on the relief, a small dinner was arranged in the lighthouse with a few of Lundy's invited guests. The framed ode was given to Ken after a splendid meal and he was well pleased. Other small gifts were received and a few bottles of wine made the evening a success. What disturbed me about what happened was that Ken, a strict disciplined Principal Keeper, was so taken with what was written he actually cried. A grown man in tears is not perhaps unusual but in Ken's case, it was embarrassing as Ken's character was stiff upper lip and matter of fact.

The party finally broke up and the guests departed for home, and the clearing up was completed before my middle watch routine. Ken departed on the helicopter for his last time and retirement and we settled down and got back to normal. The following month, a letter arrived addressed to myself from Ken's good lady wife saying that Ken was so touched by the splendid send off and the framed ode was hung on the living room wall in pride of place. She went on to say he was ecstatic about his farewell party and I am writing to say a very big thank you for making his leaving memorable.

Operational Instructions in the Small Room

Item 1.

If the door is closed, this probably means that somebody has already beaten you to it and some restraint and even patience will have to be exercised whilst business is being done.

Item 2.

After ascertaining that the appliance is now free, have you first checked that the landing area is completely clear and nobody is working near the outlet pipe. This could save considerable embarrassment and I do think fellow keepers and personnel would be most appreciative.

Item 3.

After compliance with item 2, you have checked the landing area and on your return from the gallery the door is now closed. It just might be possible that somebody has yet again beaten you to it and an authoritative knock upon the door will establish if yet further restraint is necessary; failure to knock on the door could result in a lavatory brush being used for a purpose for which it was never designed.

Item 4.

Flushing after business (big jobs only) would be appreciated, it just may result in the bowl not being completely cleared, this of course depends on the quantity deposited. Patience will once again have to be exercised whilst the cistern refills and the time spent waiting could be used to great effect by poking the offending jobbies around the bend. Please do use the tools provided and not your hands as this will help to keep the door handles clean. A second flushing now will usually ensure that all that is left is a lingering smell which can be soon remedied anyway by opening the window and leaving the door ajar.

Item 5.

The wee small room is once more than ready for new business. I do thank you for your kind assistance in this very delicate matter and I think the keepers will be most thankful. Reading these instructions whilst sitting comfortably means that at least you don't have to contemplate a study of your naval.

Party Present

It's fair to say that even at my most patronising, I am to many a jolly good egg and an absolute must for any party; I am usually first on everyone's list whatever the occasion. Sally's party invitation for the coming Saturday saying I had simply had to be there was a considerable boost to my self-esteem. It was certainly a step up amongst my friends and the local party patrons. An invitation to their celebration was a real breakthrough. Sally's and Dennis' bashes were legendary. Mind my surprise at the timing of this party was somewhat confusing as a divorce had been on the cards for simply ages, but had been put off several times for the sake of the animals. An accumulation of so many animals, dogs, cats, rabbits, gerbils and a tortoise, Dennis, I fear, was considered way down the list of priorities for Sally's considerations.

My month ashore from the lighthouse duty period was I thought at the time a blessing as a Trinity House bash is an occasion not to be missed. But at long last, it was now official, Sally was launching her newfound status with a champagne knees up before the house was vacated and put on the market. I was really chuffed to think that I was one of the chosen. The only snag as far as I could see was what should I take along as a party gift or present, what would be appropriate. Local gift shops, boutiques and markets produced not a single good idea and I was beginning to think that my wanderings, looking, were in vain. Merchandise even in the summer months was mostly uninspiring and I thought that there was no easy solution. What I wonder will I have to do, something I suppose will turn up eventually.

The Sunday paper supplement proved to be the answer; my eye espied an item advertising reproduction chastity belts, perfect replicas made in cast iron, complete with its very own padlock and key. I sent off a cheque and awaited delivery. Time was getting short but it duly arrived in readiness for the party.

When presented to Sally on the night of the party, its reception, I must say, proved all I could have hoped for. "Oh what an unusual present," she said, "do look everybody." Her face was a picture; I do believe she was honestly appreciative.

Now it must be explained that Sally is a women of ample proportions, some would say large, everything moves but not necessarily in unison with her tiny feet, a pulled in tight belt seemed to extenuate the body mass but body wobble was not restricted, it seemed to move with a mind of its own.

"Do come and have a look, Alfredo," she said. Now it seems that Alfredo was the new apple of Sally's eye and I did wonder where Dennis was but obviously things had moved on at a pace and as Dennis was nowhere to be seen, Alfredo was now flavour of the month. Alfredo was a ski instructor at the new sports centre. The dry ski run necessitating the importing of a qualified person to fill this post, why a Spanish fellow who didn't speak hardly any English was employed, I couldn't fathom out but obviously, Sally and he once introduced were smitten, love blossomed over numerous hot chocolates in the sports centre cafeteria. Skiing, given Sally's size, was out of the question but keep fit classes enabled the two to get together frequently.

Alfredo's lack of understanding of the English language and total bemusement of what a chastity belt was for, was I feel partly to blame for what followed at the party.

Sally held aloft for everybody to see how pleased she was with the gift. "Isn't it absolutely fabulous?" she squealed.

"Why don't you try it on?" said an already tipsy neighbour. I think by the look of him he had already been dipping his glass into the punch bowl twice as much as anybody else.

"I will!" she yelled and swinging the chastity belt above her head, she proceeded to the bedroom saying, "give me five minutes and I will see if it fits."

I wallowed in the adulation of my fellow guests. "Such a clever idea," they said, "brilliant, knockout, you really must come to our next party get together."

Sally's later return quietened the party proceedings, and she announced to all and sundry. "It fits like a glove as if it was made for me," she beamed constantly, what a super present.

When the whoops and cheers had died down, Sally clapped her hands and said that she had an announcement to make so could we all have a bit of peace and quiet. She moved to Alfredo's side and after a hefty cuddle said that she and Alfredo had married that very morning at the local registry office and this party was now the wedding celebration.

A moments gaping then loud whoops and cheers greeted this sudden turn of events. Much backslapping and congratulations from all the assembled guests followed with a rush to replenish empty glasses to toast the happy couple. The music volume was turned up and dancing proceeded at a livelier pace. So when an hour or so later, Sally came quivering over to my side, I was more than on top form, she said she was off shortly to change into her going away gear and can she please have the key to the chastity belt padlock. "Well, I suppose you had better have it especially on your wedding night."

After searching my pockets for the missing key, I was comprehending the full meaning of that expression. Suddenly turning cold sober, I could feel the whole room cooling, slowly all conversation died, the music was stopped and all eyes turned to me as I patted each pocket time after time; this was repeated even inside out pocket linings were searched but all to no avail. Where the hell was the key? Oh dear.

"Now surely," said the now proper drunken neighbour finally, "don't you have a spare key."

"Well if you think about it," I said, "there is only supposed to be the one key. That's the whole point. What a carry on. Have you got a file, Sally?" I said and proceeded to the bathroom clutching the ugly file in my hand. I don't suppose it would have taken me more than five minutes to free the chastity belt but suddenly, the door was shouldered open by Alfredo and finding myself in a most embarrassing position didn't make for friendly relations. I suppose in the circumstances of my kneeling in front of his new wife and a horrid rasping noise, it isn't the best of circumstances to be found in.

Alfredo is a powerful man; skiing has kept him fit but banging my head against the lavatory bowl and sending me sprawling on the floor did seem overzealous, and two teeth plopped down into the lavatory pan and disappeared. Clutching my bloodied face, I was manhandled to the living room and a chair was cleared so that first aid could be administered. Gawping guests by this time had materialised and further confusion was not helped by overly heated explanations especially as translation into Spanish was at best muddled.

Well as they do say, it's all water now under the bridge and I am not really complaining and very soon I will be back on eating solids again. Sally and Alfredo did send me a box of soft fruits as a token of the embarrassment by all concerned, but I suppose time will eventually mend my swollen face, but missing teeth, that is something else. What's beyond doubt is that my partying days are diminished as invites to parties just don't happen anymore. I wonder why? Was it something I said? The key was never found and I am sure that I had better not ask how the honeymoon night went.

Percy, the Seagull

Round Island is the most northerly of the Scilly Lighthouses. It is perched on a massive island of granite rock. Because of its location between the Seven Stones and the Lightship guarding, this reef it is most important for shipping in the South-Western approaches. The Torrey Canyon disaster that was wrecked on this reef spilling millions of gallons of oil is testament to its importance.

I was stationed on Round Island Lighthouse for a number of years, in fact right through its transformation to becoming automatic. Percy, the seagull, was a constant companion for most of those years. Percy was a one-legged herring gull who was such a cheeky chap that he would eat out of your hand. He hopped to and fro on his good leg along the whole perimeter of the surround wall until he was fed. Usually by the morning watchman. All the food scraps were saved for this purpose. I must say that there was never much food left over but what there was, Percy greedily tucked into his gullet. With his handicap of having only one leg, I expect he found scrounging from the keepers easier than having to work at fishing for his grub. His comical bobbing and hopping about, I think, played a big part in gaining the keepers sympathy. He was a smart bird; even other seagulls would try and muscle in on his territory, but he always saw them off.

Ken, the Principal Keeper, was on the morning watch routine and having had his breakfast, Percy was waiting for the left overs, his usual antics always brought a reward and Ken put the offerings on the wall. Percy stuffed them away and flew off to his normal roost to regurgitate and devour at his leisure. Ken, doing the business in the engine room, returned to see Percy in the open window of the kitchen and he had Ken's false teeth in his beak. The bright sunny morning had meant that the window was thrown wide and Ken's usual early morning shower and clean-up had been completed and the teeth were always put in a glass of water with steradent tablets for a good soak, and left on the window. Ken was proud of his sparkling toothy smile but he would never be caught without his teeth missing, as top and bottom were always back in place when in company. Gummy without the teeth just wasn't right. He shouted at Percy to leave the teeth alone and even went in search of a slice of bread to entice him to drop his molars, but Percy was having none of it. His normal roost on the adjoining Island (St Helen's) meant he was out of reach. Ken watched in anger as the bird tossed them up in the air time and time again to try and break them into manageable pieces to swallow.

When we were in the kitchen later with Ken, he said to us that Percy was not to be fed ever again; he was not to be trusted. Poor old Ken was a sight with his gummy smile and when dinner meal time arrived, he struggled manfully but it was a real trial. Percy, I think perhaps, realised that there were no more easy pickings at Round Island and soon disappeared completely. He probably found sympathy at St Mary's Island. Ken's return for his next month's duty sporting a brand-new set of teeth produced a smile all around with his new teeth gnashers but from now on, his teeth in a glass was always left in the bathroom.

Pulling the Pot

Highlight of the day is the pulling of the lobster pot, will we be dining on fresh crab sandwiches or perhaps even a nice lobster. Probably, it will be jam butties again. I have always wondered why on asking my keeping colleagues about who will help in catching bait or cooking the crabs or even picking out the crabmeat. There are never any volunteers until the question is asked, who would like lobster or crab for tea, everybody puts their hand up.

The drawing of the pot from the murky depths always ensures the gathering of the full crew to see what bounty comes forth from the sea. Once again, on inspection, there was nothing but a small weaver fish and even the precious bait was eaten. The small, little fish was opening and closing its mouth as if to say throw us back mate and in its final death throes, it gave one last mighty leap and smacked the Principal Keeper on his sit upon (backside). The Principal Keeper, although a large fellow, jumped and gave a shout and made such a noise about it that I wondered what all the fuss was about. The fish was kicked back into the sea and was seen to swim away. The Principal Keeper rushed into the lighthouse clutching his backside and cursing all and sundry. Falling about laughing about the Principal Keeper's antics, the lobster pot was stowed away and when more bait could be caught, we will have to try yet again.

We proceeded to the kitchen bemoaning our wasted efforts with the pot to be greeted with an awesome sight. The Principal Keeper was stood on a chair with his trousers around his ankles positioning a mirror the better to see the inflamed area that the weaver fish had inflicted on his bum. The scene was so funny that both Keepers fell about in fits of laughter once again, further hysterics followed when he asked if perhaps some soothing cream could be applied. What an awesome sight, enough to put you off your grub for life.

Clearly, the pain was not to be laughed at and the Principal Keeper stormed out of the kitchen and said he was off to bed. This suggestion was easy to make, as it would save further embarrassment and give time to look up the remedy for treatment.

The weaver fish (dragon) has poisonous dorsal spines which can inflict a very nasty wound. The lesser weaver fish, although just as poisonous, proves usually not to be fatal. But like all fishy stories, how big was our fish?

We, of course, couldn't take the chance and medical advice was obviously required as both Assistant Keepers didn't know what treatment was to be administered. The hospital was contacted and the doctor explained that the poison could be sucked out of the infected area as soon as possible then bathed and covered with a light dressing. We thanked the doctor and broke radio contact and proceeded to the bedroom. Both looking shame faced, we imparted the glad tidings to the Principal Keeper, that there was good news and bad news. He did look terrible and he had an awfully high temperature and was moaning and groaning like a big jessie. We told him the good news first, the doctor said the pain only lasts for a short period of time. He brightened up on hearing this and asked what the bad news was. There is no known cure and you will probably be dead by morning.

Is this story true or possibly just a good opportunity for poking fun at our glorious leader, I will leave you to decide. What was the size of the weaver fish? Well, he did recover finally.

Rules for Visiting Personnel

When visiting personnel are on station at a Lighthouse, certain rules and working practices must be implemented as the station routine must continue in an orderly and satisfactory fashion. The rules should be digested and followed where possible, or the full consequences or deviation from the rules will be met with dire reprisals from the Lighthouse Keepers.

Rule 1.

Upsetting the Keepers is a definite no, no. Not allowed or encouraged.

Rule 2.

Bribing of Keepers is allowed (cream buns, chocolate biscuits, sweeties, alcoholic drink). Any of these is most acceptable.

Rule 3.

Cooking of succulent steaks too frequently in front of poorly paid Keepers is a definite misdemeanour as this selfish practise can cause ill feeling. Offer to share perhaps, or suffer the consequences. Cut thin spam is the usual fare for Keepers, so be warned.

Rule 4.

Smelly socks and shoes in the tower bedroom is a very fundamental problem and is considered taboo. Remedial work to rectify this unsavoury problem is to occasionally wash, or leave your shoes and socks outside of the bedroom. If none compliance, collecting your shoes and socks from the sea after an irate keeper has thrown them out of the window might be difficult.

Rule 5.

Dishes will be washed by the keepers for you, but stop and think is it worth having soapy washing water splashed down your back or a dish mop dropped into your lap. The obvious conclusion is that it's easier to do your own dishes or perhaps even offer to do the Keepers pots pans as well as your own.

Rule 6.

The Principal Keeper's chair is definitely off limits. On no account attempt to use this chair as black looks. Stomping of feet and tantrums are shore to follow. It's far easier to humour than to antagonise. It makes for a more peaceful life.

Rule 7.

The Principal Keeper's word is law, but it do make sense to first check with the other keepers, two against one means democracy at work should ensure the assistants are always right.

Rule 8.

Do try and be quiet on station as any visitor or workman who is deemed to be noisy, will have retaliatory reprisals. The fog signal will blast his sleeping hours right through the night.

Rule 9.

The television is controlled by the keeper on watch but can be persuaded to switch to your favourite programme with a hefty bribe (as in Rule 2).

Rule 10.

Wearing dirty overalls in the living quarters is not very sensible. Oil and grease on the easy chairs is a sure way of upsetting the keepers. Retaliatory consequences are the banning of all wanted television programmes and the forced having to endure EastEnders and Coronation Street each night.

Rule 11.

Don't be a measurable moaner, we know being marooned on a tower Lighthouse is not everybody's idea of paradise but grin and bear it. Think of all the money you are saving by not being down the pub supping beer. The money saved will probably be spent by your wife anyway by the time you get home again.

Rule 12.

Games that are played on Lighthouses such as Chess, Scrabble, cards and you are lucky to be invited to participate, please remember to play in the right true spirit. Continually winning is a very foolish practise, as this will almost certainly result in some sort of retaliatory reprisals. A shaking of an opponent's hand at the conclusion of any game is much appreciated, but beware of spiteful hand crushers.

A/ Foreign bodies in your nightly beverage.

B/ Hovering whilst trying to watch television.

C/ Fog signal whilst trying to sleep.

D/ Any of the above for persistent smart-asses.

Don't be naughty, do follow the rules, behave and follow the code. If you think the rules are somewhat biased towards the Keepers, you could possibly be right, but least line of resistance usually wins in the end.

Safety and Survival Course

Since helicopters have been introduced to do the reliefs to some of the most inaccessible Lighthouses, it has much improved. The relief is done on the day and if you are going ashore after a duty period, it's usually done without any fuss, unless there is fog. In the past with boat reliefs, you could be days or even weeks waiting for favourable sea conditions. The biggest hazard is fog; you can't fly and sometimes although it's most frustrating, but remembering boat reliefs soon brings everything back into perspective.

The government rules state that all personnel flying over water by helicopter must attend a safety survival-training course, every two years. Pass and you can fly to comply with the safety regulations. My biannual safety course was to be held at Lowestoft Maritime college, I was not looking forward to it one little bit as the stories about the dreaded dunker are legion. Being a reasonable swimmer, I don't mind being on top of the water but beneath the sea has no appeal for me at all.

The Probable and theory lessons I listened to with full attention so that when the practical had to be put into practise, I would be ready. The day arrived when the test was to be carried out. Twelve keepers each with their own misgivings presented themselves at the poolside of the college. Boiler suits were issued to wear over swimming trunks and plimsolls for footwear; this was explained as being necessary to simulate the actual conditions should you be ditched into the sea. After selecting a life jacket and checking the correct wearing and tying, you are asked to climb up onto the high platform above the pool. The estimated height of this platform was about 26ft, but it certainly looked higher prior to jumping.

The instructor asked me to stand on the edge of the platform in readiness to jump when so instructed. Why I was chosen to be first, I don't know, but I was asked if I was ready, and he said that one hand should be used to close off the nasal passages and the other hand should be crossed over to hold the lifejacket in place to stop it riding up when entering the water and smacking you in the kisser. "All ready," he asked again, "then jump."

I stepped off the platform into the void, it seemed like ages before I entered the water feet first, an almighty jolt I received to my wedding tackle brought instant tears to my eyes, when I broke water back to the surface, I could see the class all grinning and laughing and even the instructor couldn't keep a straight face. He shouted for quiet and said that is not the way to do it. Perhaps I should have told you to keep your feet together or you could get a nasty jolt to your privates. Why he couldn't have told me before I jumped, I just don't know. Three times this exercise was completed but the lesson learnt of keeping my feet together was followed each time. A different exercise was tagged on whilst we were in the water. Jumping into the water and swimming into a group to get into a twelve-man life raft followed. Towing a fellow keeper, the entire length of the pool and climbing a wire ladder was another exercise. Righting the large life raft so that it fell back onto your face and pushed you under water again without getting tangled in the ropes was made doubly difficult because of the lifejackets buoyancy. The swimmers in our group, I have the upmost respect for, as they all were all put through the same procedures whether they could swim or not. The whole time that we were in the water on these exercises, I did wonder if constant spraying with a hosepipe was necessary, but was told that if this was at sea, this is what you would expect. Simulation of the conditions was essential.

One of the safety attendants was a young girl called Samantha, she was asked to show everyone how the dunker worked. She and another colleague were strapped into the cage seats and the safety straps fastened in nice and tight. The whole contraption was turned upside down and started to sink to the bottom of the pool. The water came up to their necks and slowly, all the air was forced out, both inside took a last gulp of air and disappeared to the bottom. Both soon reappeared in a short space of time.

"Now who wants to be in the first group?" Nobody spoke and a deathly hush descended. "Come on you lot, if a young slip of a girl can do it so can you surely?" I did notice that Samantha was swimming the length of the pool mostly underwater, just like a water nymph. Six teams of two were chosen and each time a diver would be going into the dunker with us with breathing apparatus. Safety helmets were dished out blue for swimmers and red for those who couldn't swim. Nose pegs could be worn if required. No lifejackets were needed as you will stick to the ceiling (floor upside down). My turn as usual was first in line. I was strapped into my seat with a red helmet fellow who couldn't swim next to me but what I did make sure about was that I was next to the door and in control of the opening door handle. You are only as quick as the person next to you and if he was to panic, I was also going to be trouble. We were turned upside down after the water level rose from around my feet to the ceiling and the air pocket got smaller and smaller, I took a last mouth of fresh air before we were dropped to the pool floor. The seat belts were soon undone and the diver made a sign to get out of the door and swim to the surface, I didn't need telling twice. Out I shot and I wish I had used a nose peg as I was coughing and sputtering when I surfaced, my colleague soon followed in much the same condition. *Well, thank goodness that's done.* When all six sets of keepers had been through the dunking process without any mishaps, the instructor said that he was well pleased and if anybody would like a second go in the dunker again, please step forward, nobody moved of course.

Certificates were issued the next day and first aid courses began but thank goodness, we didn't have to worry about the dunker for another two years.

SARK

Sark is the smallest of the Channel Island group of Lighthouses. Its location is between Jersey and Guernsey; Alderney is situated only six miles from the French coast of Cap de la Hague. Sark is only about two miles long and three miles wide. The beautiful cliffs and scenery makes it a paradise for quiet walks and relaxation. No cars or traffic problems as the only mode of transport is cycles. Horse and carts meet the ferryboat (Ile de Sark) and transport them to the top of the Island. The landing quay is most impressive; an arch through the rock enables passengers to climb the steep path to the top. When I arrived to take up station, I was met by one of my fellow keepers who helped with my baggage and stores.

Although the lighthouse is classed as a rock (month on month off), it's a wonderful posting. My trip out from Guernsey was a good passage and I was looking forward to the chance of exploring the Island. The watch routine was soon established and my off-duty periods, I was told I could spend as I liked. The small collection of wooden shops was certainly different; there was a bakery a butcher and a collection of gift shops. The bike hire shop was run by an ex-keeper who fell in love with the Island and stayed. The Principal Keeper was fond of partaking of a few beers and as the pub never closed, he was in clover. The lighthouse bicycle I used constantly to explore the whole Island. A bakery fresh made French stick, a hunk of cheese with a bottle of wine and I was in heaven.

The Island populace, a very small community, soon made themselves known and I was invited to attend the Whist drive on Tuesdays and euchre drives on Thursdays. Where this coincided with the Lighthouse duty, both keepers were always most obliging to cover for me as long as a swap was in place. The boys on the Island played football most weeks and were always short of players and I was asked to help out even if it was only in goal. The after-game comradery in the pub afterwards was well worth the effort.

Daily visitors to the Island often dropped in to see the Lighthouse and were most welcome. The keeper on watch was expected to show them around and of course, appreciation in the form of donations placed in the hat helped to pay for the beers. I did wonder one afternoon when the Principal Keeper offered visitors a glass of gin and orange. It was gratefully accepted and when they had gone, I asked where he had produced that from as I didn't know he had any gin. "That wasn't gin, that was white methylated spirit. You could hardly tell the difference when mixed with loads of orange." He meant well but it was just a bit naughty. White methylated spirits are used to clean the lens of course.

When it was my turn to show the visitors around, a family party of ten people wanted to see the tower. I showed them around and when they climbed up into the lantern galley, the mother froze, the glass glazing reaches to the gallery floor and as the Lighthouse is perched on the side of the cliff, her legs gave way and she clung on to the glazing and collapsed. The sheer drop over the side of the cliff is I suppose daunting, but trying to explain that to the woman produced little reaction. Luckily, I was right behind her as she climbed into the lantern and caught her as she fell, but her large size and weight was a real problem. The family thought it funny, but I could see the panic in her face. "Close your eyes," I said, and man-handled her down the vertical ladder with her husband's help. *The brass handrails would take some cleaning*, I thought, and a cup of sweet tea soon had the women back to normal. My month's duty was all too soon over but I would go back at any time, it certainly beats the Wolf Rock.

Sod's Law

After a wonderful day at the Dartmouth Regatta, complete with an air display from the Red Arrows and a Grand Regatta fireworks show seen from the river aboard the Dartmouth ferry, the last thing that was wanted was a stubborn air lock keeping everybody awake all night, especially the adjoining neighbours. The fair, the beer and the whole day's activities was somewhat overshadowed by the calamitous events that followed such a wonderful day.

When we arrived home, a troublesome pipe with an air lock had suddenly developed a loud banging noise. This problem had suddenly materialised after a new shower had been fitted, several attempts at clearing this nagging occurrence over the previous week had been solved by turning on the water taps; this always seemed to cure it but obviously, the plumber needed to come back which was scheduled for the Monday morning. Sod's law. Running the water usually cleared the air lock and the banging pipes ceased and all was returned to normal, but not tonight.

Perhaps my inebriated state had something to do with the frustrating sequence of events but Sod's law I think played a major part. Well past midnight, nearer one o'clock, a loud banging could be heard in the water tank pipes coming from the attic, this was followed shortly by next doors window being thrown open and the irate neighbours shouting to stop the offending banging noise. The language that was used didn't allow for an argument and my shouted response was in assurance rather than in confrontation, I did think, however, that naughty words like that were most unbecoming of a lady, understandable in the circumstances but not very helpful.

My first action was to turn on the water taps which should have offered a quick cure, but on turning the taps back off again, the banging once more started up, but with even more renewed vigour. Water taps on again and nothing for it but to get up into the attic. My fuzzy state of mind and befuddled brain and the lateness of the hour didn't make for logical thinking. The ball cock could be heard bouncing and the vibrating pipes had to be silenced. Dressed in only my skidders as the visiting family had meant vacating my own bedroom, my slippers or dressing gown would have been helpful but I suppose I will have to make do without them. A stepladder from the downstairs outhouse was the first requirement and of course a light for the attic. The fixed light in the attic unfortunately was a casualty of the plumber's overzealous antics with the copper pipe when putting in the shower unit and as yet, no replacement had been fitted. *Serves me right*, I thought, I had meant to do it but had not gotten around to it.

A screw type bulb was what was wanted but why there are so many different fittings I just don't know, nothing is ever made easy. A torch was found but the batteries on switching on soon proved that they had long ago given up the ghost and glowed for all of five seconds. A candle was the answer but where were they, in the back of the cupboard somewhere but after rummaging for ages could I find one, could I heck. The only candle was a comic scented figurine which was a lovely 'lily of the valley', that will just have to do. Matches proved even harder to find than the candle and after a fruitless search, I eventually stopped long enough to realise that I could get a light off the gas stove which was self-lighting. The figurine candles wick for some reason had burnt low into the candle making holding the candle over the flame somewhat tricky, my fingers stood up to it rather well considering my rising temper but a danger level was fast approaching. A sharp knife cutting off the figurines head cured that little problem as the wick was now fully exposed. A rolled-up newspaper spool saved my fingers from further burning and it seemed a good idea at the time but the smoke alarm battery soon showed that at least it was in a good healthy condition and the alarm didn't like burning paper. A chair was fetched and the battery removal stopped the high-pitched screeching. More burnt paper later the candle was at last alight. Candle wax was applied to a saucer to fix the candle by its base so that it wouldn't topple over. The running taps whilst still holding the banging taps at bay had been unfortunately cascading water over the washbasin rim, perhaps it might have been better to have removed the plug completely out of the way and well clear before departing downstairs.

A large pool and a sodden carpet greeted my return. *Oh dear, another mess to clear up.* I whipped the plug belatedly with such force out of the way that it fell into the lavatory bowl. After retrieving the plug, I noticed that someone had failed to pull the flush, the dirty blighters, a quick wash of my hand was now a priority. The taps were turned off at this point and I thought I would clear up the water later. The ladder was positioned to climb into the attic and with my candle in hand, the hatch was lifted. The troublesome ballcock will be silenced once and for all. Feeling with my bare feet for the rafters, I progressed slowly towards the water tank, I did wonder why water tanks always seem to be put so far away from the access space opening, *never mind, just get on with it.*

The insulation fibreglass laid across the beams and rafters was somebody's lazy way to insulate the roof space but it made the location of foot holds almost impossible to find. I overcame this problem by sliding my foot along the rafters and inching my way towards the tank. Rough unplanned wood soon produced a loud curse as a splinter embedded itself in my foot, and bringing my foot quickly back for a closer inspection in the candle light showed a great big splinter sticking out with a seemingly an ever-increasing amount of blood. Balancing on one leg and holding onto the candle in my precarious position, I, of course, overbalanced. Putting out my hand which held the candle, the inevitable happened, it slid off the saucer and I was once more plunged in total darkness. Blast, dam and double blast or words to that effect. It was at this point that the tank now having refilled itself that the banging pipes started up again. Hell, now I was really wound up. I clambered back towards the access hatch and jumped from the ladder to the floor, a shout from my occupied bedroom to keep the noise down I didn't respond to as I didn't trust what I thought putting into words would be helpful. The banging was stopped by turning on the taps again, but I did make sure no plug was stopping the water going down the plughole. I did notice that my blood patches now mingled with the water along the carpet, perhaps first thing should be to remove the slinter. A pair of tweezers from downstairs soon had the splinter removed and a sticking plaster to stop the flow of blood over the wound was applied. Still no more candles, so back to the attic to search for the figurine. Repeating the whole process of lighting the candle again after retrieving it from the attic was making my blood boil.

When once more back into the attic with the candle, I methodically inched my way to the water tank. Who had insulated the roof space had made a very good job of covering the water tank, it was completely covered, don't people know that access was required in an emergency? The covering was ripped to shreds in my frenzy, I eventually laid bare the wooden cover and the ball cock was at last accessible. Both hands were needed to bend the stupid arm back nearly in half, a little bit of overkill perhaps, but I wasn't taking any chances. A length of string was tied around the bent arm so that no water could again start the banging, the plumber will just have to sort it all out; it was, after all, his fault in the first place.

What a day, don't you just wonder sometimes how it is that simple little things have a habit of ganging up on you and making mischief, Sod's Law I suppose.

Spring Lambs

Spring is in the air and it's a bright and beautiful day as I take my walk towards the Marisco Tavern on Lundy Island having secured my day off from watch keeping at the Lighthouse at Lundy South. A brisk walk listening to the skylark high in the sky, singing his merry song. A well-earned pint and perhaps even a pasty, of course it depends on what's been cooked. No ship today with loads of visitors from the mainland at Bideford, the 'Oldenburge' is not due till tomorrow.

My knapsack on my back and my strong walking boots upon my feet urges me onward across the island with not a care in the world. I have even got my trusty viper stick just in case. I am often asked if this fearsome weapon on Lundy is really necessary, but as I say to they that ask, although I have never yet seen an adder on Lundy it's probably because the long 'v' cleft stick always frightens them away. Better to be safe than sorry.

Perhaps I should have timed it better as I will just about catch the tavern before it closes at lunchtime. Spring lambs is one of life's little pleasures, new born on shaky legs with tails twitching playfully, hopping and jumping around the other ewes, it's a sight that never fails to gladden the heart. The field between quarter wall and halfway wall is divided into two large fields with an electric fence down the middle. The first thing I notice as I come to the farm gate is that at least a dozen or so lambs are the wrong side of the electric fence and bleating for their lost mothers. New born and obviously in some distress, how they managed to get the wrong side is a mystery. *This isn't right*, so I thought I would reunite the dear lambs with the rest of the flock.

I rounded up the little lambs with the help of my adder catcher and pushed them towards the gate, but when I was at the gate, I found that the gate opened towards me, so that the lambs jumped around and shot off across the field again. *Oh dear, this is no good, as I will just have to start again. Think about it,* I thought to myself, *and perhaps if I left the gate just open a little bit then when I have got them rounded up they can go into the next field and be back where they belong.*

A flanking operation was needed and as soon as I was anywhere near the little blighters, they scarpered further away. I was not to be beaten and eventually, I managed to get them running in the right direction towards the gate. This was taking an almighty long time and I was concerned that my pint was probably now long gone as the Tavern closing time was well past. When I thought I had everything under control, I saw to my amazement that the open gate was now awash with a white tide of sheep, where one went, like sheep they all followed. Which field had the most sheep in I couldn't say and trying to stem the flood of sheep on the move was an impossibility. I did chase about for a considerable time trying to put right the trouble I seemed to have caused. My running about was getting me nowhere.

I realised there was nothing I could do about the two fields of sheep instead of the one, so I had better go and catch the farmer, *I don't think he will be pleased.* John was having his dinner when I called and he listened to my tales of woe and his face showed his understanding of the problem. "Why don't you stick to lighthouse keeping," he said, "and leave farming to they that know?"

We marched back to the fields after John had finished his dinner and he called Bess, the collie sheep dog, to his side. The way all the sheep were herded up and returned to the proper field was what I thought miraculous, especially in such a short space of time. When we parted, I was told in no uncertain way to keep to what I do best, and a pint or two would be appreciated for the trouble I had caused. I trudged back to the lighthouse and not a sniff of a pint, I had well and truly had my knuckles rapped. Each to their own I suppose, a hard lesson learned.

The Christmas Cake

The Wolf Rock lighthouse is situated about halfway between the rocks of Land's End and the Isles of Scilly. Tides and currents around this tower rock are not for the unwary. South Westerly seas tend to build up for most of the winter months straight across from America and the first thing the sea encounters is the Wolf. Huge waves hit and roar on to the Land's End outcrop and spring back off the rocks to meet the next South Westerly. When both sets of waves arrive together at the Wolf Rock Lighthouse, the white water is forced up and over the top, because the tower is over 100ft, it makes for very careful watch keeping. It's probably the least favourite of lighthouses to be posted too.

Christmas on board is not very popular as all keepers want to be home with the family, but with a month on and a month off duty, it's inevitable that everybody gets a turn. Bob decided to go sick for Christmas, (jammy devil), I just hope it's something serious. Because of this shortfall of the three keepers, a pool keeper was assigned.

A giant of a man from the Yorkshire dales called Les, he wasn't well pleased to miss his Christmas at home, but duty calls, so grin and bear it as they say. We met for the first time whilst packing our store of food to cover the month whilst on board. Penzance depot the day before relief was a hive of activity as all the keepers from the other lighthouses were packing their gear as well. The reliefs all take place by helicopter from Sennen Cove on the following day which is just around the corner from Land's End. Longships, Seven Stones Lightship, Bishop Rock, Round Island all the crews were busy getting ready for their stint of duty. It was pointed out to the new guy from the pool that as it was Christmas, the three on our crew usually club together to make Christmas special, cooped up and away from family and friends is hard enough anyway. Les said that he would treat it just like another period of duty, no special treats and no, he did not want to be part of our normal arrangement. "What no turkey, no beer or even a bottle of wine, mince pies or even crackers. No stuff that," he said. "If I am away, then I will treat it just the same as normal." The rest of the crews looked on in amazement and couldn't believe a whole month spent with this surly fellow would end well.

"How about a drink with the crews down the pub when the packing is weighed and finished, as it's the last chance whilst ashore?"

"No thank you, it's of no interest, I would sooner have a wander around." Oh dear, some joyous times ahead.

The relief was done and Christmas was still some time ahead, so settling in and waving a cheery goodbye to the opposite crew it soon reached a routine. The beer was stashed in the recess window outside of the kitchen landing and the turkey was in the freezer, all in readiness for Christmas.

Christmas day I was morning watch (0400–1200) so it was me for cooking duties. The turkey had been taken out of the freezer and all that remained was to make sure the vegetables were made ready. Beer and wine chilling nicely, even paper napkins and crackers would be brought into use. The solid fuel stove was showing plenty of heat as threatening the Principle Keeper to stoke it well in his middle watch had paid dividends. Breakfast was a bit of a struggle as telephone conversations over the radio with loved ones seemed to take forever. The appointed time for the festive dinner had arrived; the table was set and as it was Christmas turkey with all the trimmings and cocktail sausages wrapped in bacon was served to all three keepers. Well, it is Christmas. Christmas pudding with brandy sauce followed. Crackers were pulled and the silly hats were worn. All in all, a splendid dinner. The wine glasses were filled (three) and the cans of beer evenly distributed. Most agreeable and everybody turned to wash up and clear the dishes. After my morning watch duty, it was me for a couple of hours sleep and a call at tea time. The tea was ready and three mince pies were heated and put on the table and it was said that what a pity we had forgotten a Christmas cake. So many other bits and pieces but this item was missed. Les at this point said that his wife had given him a cake for Christmas and proceeded to his store cupboard and produced a large tin. The lid came off and the Christmas cake was centred on the table. A kitchen knife was fetched and a large wedge of cake was cut, the paper frills had to be peeled back and the removal of the snowman and robin from the icing was soon done. Why only one plate and one slice, the Principle Keeper and I watched in total disbelief as the cake was returned into the cake tin and put away in his cupboard. I did say to Les that I thought the Christmas cake looked wonderful. "Yes," he said, "it should be as my wife is a good cook and this is a treat every time I am away from home. Well, I never. Do you fancy some cold turkey and pickles for supper some boiled ham, how about another beer, but do be careful and make sure it's only for the two of us mind Les can make do with his cake? I have seen it all now, I know it's Christmas but there are limits. Hurry back Bob, and let's get back to our normal crew."

The Eddystone Lighthouse Relief

My first appointment after serving several years as a Supernumerary Keeper was to the Eddystone Lighthouse. I was more than pleased as now at least I could look forward to some stability in my life as constantly being sent to different stations with little time at home was at an end. Month off and month on station, this meant that not knowing when I will be home were at an end. The day before the relief, I met Ginger Mutton on the Barbican. Ginger was the boatman responsible for taking me out to the Lighthouse on the following day. He asked for a list of my food requirements and with some sensible suggestions, promised to have everything ready for the early morning start. The digs that the keepers usually used was pointed out and I settled down to a good evening meal before a night out around the Barbican pubs. Not too many pints but enough to last till I came ashore in a months' time.

Early morning saw me on the quay awaiting Ginger with the stores. His ramshackle van pulled up next to the boat and my gear soon joined the expertly packed food stores. Trinity House had also sent several items from the depot at Cowes. All was put on board. A beautiful day looked to be in the offing and Ginger his son and a third crew member soon had us under way towards the Eddystone.

I was dressed in my best Trinity House uniform, white shirt, black tie, new uniform and shiny black leather shoes. Even the brass buttons had a shine. *Create a good impression, as it's my first appointment,* I thought. The trip out to the Eddystone is quite a fair way 16 miles I believe so a brew was suggested whilst we were under way. Although the weather was calm, I did feel a little queasy and was glad when the Lighthouse was in full view. Ginger stopped the engine and the rubber inflatable was put alongside, he watched the sea as it came from around the back of the lighthouse just to gauge the strength of the waves, we waited whilst he made up his mind and contented, he signalled to the keepers on board to lower the winch gable. The winch was controlled from halfway up the tower and the other keepers were on the setoff which runs around the base of the tower. Ropes and chains had been put out in readiness. A heaving line was thrown from the inflatable and caught by a keeper. This was attached to the winch cable and the inflatable returned to the boat. The winch was reeled out and with the attached line hauled aboard. Next, a bowling hitch was fastened and I was invited to step into the loop and catch hold of the overhead rope. I had every faith in the proceedings, as Ginger you could see was a first-class seaman. The winch took in the slack and I was hoisted over the side just above the water, it did seem to me that the hoist was taking an almighty long time as I was suspended still a long way off from the set off. What happened was that my weight, now heavy on the line, was pulling the boat closer to the lighthouse. The sea got closer and I found my legs and feet dragging through the water. This continued until the winch was taking in the slack at a better angle, I was dragged off the line by willing hands but my uniform and shoes were now soaking. The keeper in charge was laughing fit to burst. He pointed to the dog steps and indicated that I should climb up into the body of the Lighthouse; my gear and the stores were passed across in no time all without mishap, nothing else got wet and a wave to the departing boat with Ginger grinning like a Cheshire cat set me wondering.

When seated around, the ray burn in the kitchen drying out and partaking of another cup of tea. The full story was told. How did I like my initiation to the Eddystone Lighthouse I was asked.

What should have happened when I stepped into the loop of rope was that there should have been a rope tied to the buoy to stop the boat being pulled towards the tower. *Oh dear, did Ginger forget perhaps, did he heck, that's the last time I trust him and he will get no more beers out of me.* My uniform soon was dried and sponged free of salt and the shoes were polished back to a good shine again, but you have got to be on your toes and put your trust in your fellow keepers, my turn will come.

The Electric Fence

The island of Lundy is awash after so much rain. Even the fields are so sodden that to stray from the beaten track known as the road is guaranteed to end with ankle deep water tugging at your every step making progress hazardous and slow, quick steps made afore your feet are ready usually ends up with you flat on your face sprawling in the mud and sheep droppings. Give yourself time to sniff the last of the summer flowers and keep upwind of the silage, I don't mind the smell myself, a whiff of silage never done any harm to anybody. You know for certain you are alive and kicking, wonderful stuff, good wholesome farmyard aroma. I do say to those people that is forever moaning about the smell, that there are people in yonder churchyard who would give their high teeth to have a whiff of that instead of just pushing up the daises.

The wind blowing west southwest fair to middling, the trouble is it don't let up for very long to give you a chance to discard those heavy outer garments. Oh, for spring and sunny days, roll on to the summer again.

The trip to the north end lighthouse across the top of the Island in the Land Rover was for a routine maintenance visit by the Principal Keeper and myself from south Lundy Lighthouse. The third Keeper remained on station whilst we were off to do the honours. Watch rotas usually dictate which keepers should make the trek across the Island, but I am sure I seem to get more than my fair share of north light visits. Flog a willing horse I suppose.

The Land Rover stopped at each gate as we progressed across the Island, I was the one unfortunately asked to jump in and out to manage the gates. Muddy puddles and thick clinging mud insured that I was soon covered from head to foot, wheel spin was totally unnecessary in the going through the gate, but impatience was one of the driver's faults, always in a rush. This in and out to open gates happens on several occasions and each time, I seem to get more splattered at each gate.

Between the village field gate and quarter wall, the fields have been divided with an electric fence, they that know if it's on or not, keep well away of course. Mostly, it's not switched on anyway but today it's humming like crazy, and you have guessed it I found out the hard way. I did wonder why the naughty driver nudged my so-called colleague as I leapt out to open the gate.

His stopping in the worst possible place right in the middle of a large puddle with mud and sheep droppings I think was deliberate. My boots soon became stuck in the clinging mire. I pulled like mad to break the suction and overbalanced, both hands shot forward to break my fall and I was pitched up against the wire fence. An almighty electric shock rippled through my body, jumping up in double quick time having lost both boots, I found myself face down in the mud. My common sense seemed to have taken the day off. I lay there in frustration at the sorry state that I was in, my boots were retrieved eventually and putting my feet back into the soggy boots meant that at least I could stand up again. A shout from the Land Rover telling me to stop messing about and open the gate was the final straw. I kicked the fence and got a further shock for my troubles, my arms and feet were tingling. Slowly and with much care, I opened the gate to allow us to proceed. Why so much muck and sheep droppings always seem to congregate adjacent to a gate opening I just don't know.

When I dragged my evil smelling, body saturated in mud to get into the Land Rover once again, I was told that perhaps I could meet the Principal Keeper at the north end, as the driver didn't want all that mess in the back of his van. They sped off before I could argue. The walk cooled my temper and the Land Rover was on the way back before I reached the North light. When he passed me again, I gave him a hard stare and shouted that my turn would come so he had better watch out.

The work at the North Lighthouse went well without any further mishaps. When the time to trek back arrived to the South Lighthouse, I told the Principal Keeper I would take a deviation round to the battery as I could do with some horse mushrooms for my tea. The Principal Keeper wanted to get back as he was on watch shortly, but he did apologise for the earlier silliness. I think he just wanted some mushrooms. After collecting a bag full, it doesn't take that many when they are as big as saucers, I travelled on to the 'Marisco' Tavern. A couple of rabbits joined the mushrooms in my backpack and wearily, I travelled homeward. The farmer shot rabbits as a way to keep the pests to a manageable level; they were always hung on a wire outside of the pub for anybody to take home.

Proper job, better than chicken and countless recipes were tried and all for free. A good shower and change of clothes was the first thing, but the rabbit stew could wait for tomorrow. Tea tonight will be horse mushrooms with some streaky bacon. I will catch up with the naughty van driver; my turn will come, but all in all, a nice enough day.

The Overdue

When at long last I was transferred to the Needles,
Where supposed overdues are a thing of the past,
So, said he, my keen mate young Jerry,
As we set sail from Yarmouth at last.

The boat trip it took us near on an hour,
The light from the lighthouse shone bright,
It was cold but a very calm morning,
With the stars, a commendable sight.

The first fortnight, the weather was gorgeous,
The relief of the first man it was due,
Sure enough, the wind was fare blowing,
As I experienced the first relief overdue.

My turn came around to go shoreward,
But the sea storm and tempest did roar,
Another relief delayed by the wild sea,
"I'll be blowed," said young Jerry, "I'm sure."

The process again was often repeated,
Time and time again we were late,
I do believe we have a Jonah on board.
It's got to be young, Jerry my old mate.

The Wolf Rock Beer

Christmas away again, I am sure the calendar has conspired against me as I was away last Christmas, it was on the Eddystone Lighthouse and I suppose because of my being transferred to the Wolf Rock Lighthouse, I had fallen into the same duty period again. Hard luck but get on with it I suppose.

Wolf at Christmas didn't inspire me but make the most of it and just make the time spent away from family and friends as comfortable as possible. I asked my keeping colleagues what was the usual form to make Christmas as enjoyable as can be managed. A shared turkey, stuffing, mince pies, Christmas cake, pudding and all the little things to make the festive period go forward for some enjoyment to compensate for being at sea. "What about some beer?" I asked, and was told that each keeper could take whatever their favourite tipple was. In my case, a couple of dozen cans of beer and a bottle of whiskey, perhaps a good quality wine for the Christmas dinner table. Each keeper agreed that just about sounded right, the Principal Keeper thought that a bottle of port with a wedge of stilton would be the crowning glory to finish things off.

The relief was two weeks before the Christmas Day and packing at the Penzance depot was in full swing in readiness for our departure the next day. All the items purchased were carefully packed including the turkey and beer. Everything was weighed and labelled with the right lighthouse destination and put ready for transportation. This was essential to make sure that your food and goodies went to the right Lighthouse or else if you got it wrong, someone at a different location would be scoffing your treasures.

Next thing was a last drink with the other crew keepers down at the Turks Head Pub, the traditional last few pints whilst ashore. The sharing of costs towards Christmas items would then be sorted out. Homeward bound to St Ives after a skin full, the wife had been arranged to pick me up from the pub at 7 o'clock but perhaps I should have made it much later as when the appointed time arrived, I was most reluctant to leave. Her perseverance and coaxing eventually got me into the car and we travelled homeward. I suppose the threat of making my own way home if I didn't hurry up and finish my beer was the deciding factor.

Day of the relief was mostly uneventful; all the lighthouses had the changeover of crews completed by helicopter, and the chance of fog was blown away with the weather, bright, crisp and sunny. It has been known for extra time ashore because of the weather and the further chance of supping a few more ales. Not today, though, my head was still recovering from last night's intake.

The relief was done and after waving a cheery farewell to the going ashore crew we settled down to a routine. The boxes of food were unpacked and stowed away; the precious stock of beer was put in the window recess to keep cool. It was agreed between the crew that as Christmas was still some time away nobody should broach the beer stock till Christmas, otherwise come the day there would be nothing left.

The Wolf Rock is notorious for strong tides and heavy seas and the South Westerly wind kicked up giving the tower a right old battering. The tower rock is built to withstand this constant onslaught and the watch keeper is forever opening and shutting different window shutters to keep the sea at bay. Windows, I might add, are about 6ft thick and made of gunmetal, as are all the casements. The seas are in the main from the southwest and as long as those windows are shuttered, the opposite north east windows can be left open without fear of the sea entering the tower.

The fateful day arrived, Christmas Eve. I arrived in the kitchen for breakfast after my middle watch duties to be met with both keepers looking most upset. "Have you noticed anything different?" I was asked.

"Have you combed your hair differently?" I said hopefully.

"No, no can't you see anything missing?"

My eyes swivelled automatically to the kitchen window where the beer should have been, it was shuttered and the sea was giving it an almighty pounding but then again, that was quite normal. "Where have you moved the beer," I asked.

"We haven't," they both replied in unison, "we haven't touched it but the blasted sea has taken the lot. Not all of it surely, how could that have happened."

The wind had changed quarters apparently on the high morning tide and whilst my watch mate had been switching the main light off and hanging the curtains, the blasted sea had plucked every can of our precious beer and dumped it into the sea. It wouldn't have been so bad perhaps if we had given into temptation and consumed some of the stock of beer, but we had not so much as had a sniff of a drink. What a waste. Foolish keepers that we were, we will have to make do with the bottle of wine and the odd tot of whiskey.

What a sober Christmas this is going to be, anyone for a small tot to drown our sorrows, we had better make sure nothing happens to this our only source of sustenance.

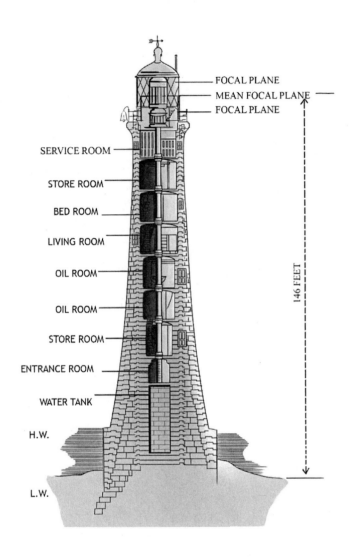

FOCAL PLANE

MEAN FOCAL PLANE

FOCAL PLANE

SERVICE ROOM

STORE ROOM

BED ROOM

LIVING ROOM

OIL ROOM

OIL ROOM

STORE ROOM

ENTRANCE ROOM

WATER TANK

H.W.

L.W.

146 FEET

Three-Legged Turkey

Christmas on Round Island Lighthouse was never going to be easy, it was my second Christmas away from home in a row, the previous Christmas I was on the Wolf Rock and because of my transfer to Round Island, the rota system had dictated that unfortunately, it was my turn yet again. *Never mind, I will just have to get on with it*, I thought, *grin and bear it.*

The relief prior to Christmas it was decided that nothing would be spared and the turkey, sausage and stuffing could be left to me and I would purchase these ashore and bring out on my relief. The cost could be worked out between the three keepers and split equally.

The turkey was found room in the freezer and could be taken out when required. My Christmas keeper colleagues, Bob and Ken, were due out on the relief two weeks after I arrived on station. I had another two weeks to go having already completed 14 days before it was my turn ashore. Ken and Bob arrived on the day of the relief which was two days before Christmas, and waving a fond cheerio to their opposite number, packing and stowing their month's goodies soon was well under way. The freezer space was cramped and a suggestion to take out the large turkey so that further space might help in getting everything in was greeted with this common-sense proposal. The turkey had to be defrosted anyway. As Christmas was almost here.

I was busy with the Christmas decorations. Cotton wool out of the first aid box provided instant snow dotted about the living quarters windows and crepe paper strips cut into festoons adorned the ceiling, holly sprigs tied together and placed in a gallon size paint tin and flashing tree lights interwoven through the branches of the aged old tinsel tree completed the not altogether displeasing sight. The folded newspaper angels were consigned to the oggin (sea) as they didn't seem to look anything like they were supposed to be, more like headless dragons really, so no angels but party balloons more than compensated.

The turkey left on the draining board was inspected and weighing in at 15lbs, everyone decided that will more than do the trick.

On Christmas morning, I was morning watch and, therefore, cook of the day. Ken and Bob were happy that I could do the honours with the cooking and the middle watch would help with the vegetables being peeled. Whilst my fellow keepers slept, I sewed an extra leg on the turkey carcass after stuffing the neck with sausage meat. The whole turkey was wrapped in mutton cloth and stuffed with an apple, a carrot with onions. A liberal coating of butter was rubbed into the turkey before placing the bird into the oven.

The morning proceeded and the constant basting in between Lighthouse duties showed and smelt beautiful. The two keepers arrived at breakfast time a little earlier than usual, as I am sure the wafting of the cooking turkey had reached their noses and enticed then to the kitchen. Breakfast done and cleared away. The dinner table was laid and Bob had even remembered to bring along a Christmas table cloth and paper napkins. The wine was cooling nicely and a plentiful supply of beer was in the fridge.

Dinnertime arrived and I asked Ken if he would like to carve whilst I contented myself with the vegetables. Well his face was a picture, the turkey with three legs; poor old Ken didn't know where to start carving. The tears of laughter trickled down his face and in the end, I pushed a glass of wine into his mitt and started on the carcass myself. "Why," they asked, "a three-legged turkey?"

"Well," I said, "you like a leg, I like a leg and I am sure Bob would like a leg. So obviously, an extra leg was required."

Time and Tide Wait for No Man

The Lighthouse on the Needles of the Isle of Wight was due for replenishment of fresh water and PGO (fuel for the engines) so the Trinity House vessel 'Patricia' was due to visit the station just two hours prior to high water, giving them plenty of time to carry out the work of filling the storage tanks. Coal was also to be delivered so that the Rayburn cooker could continue to be used for daily cooking and heating, stocks were dangerously low. Late November is not really the best of the weather to carry out these types of operations especially as the Needles Lighthouse is notorious for difficult tidal conditions, even in the summer months. The sea was not very favourable but as fuel was running low, it was decided that needs must, and the job for restocking had to be done. Common sense doesn't always apply as far as Trinity House is concerned and you have guessed it the ship had just arrived on station two hours after high water. The Lighthouse crew did wonder at the wisdom of this decision especially seeing the sea breaking over the set off. The Principal Keeper contacted the ship's commander and voiced his concern that perhaps replenishment might be better left to another day. The answer of course was as the ship was here and had dropped anchor, the workboats were already being dropped alongside and were being filled full to capacity for loading each workboat, although a sturdy enough craft built to do the heavy work, was even as we watched being tossed around by the waves. When full perhaps, the extra weight would help to stabilise the boats. The crew on each boat consisted of a cox and three workmen and a pump in its own cradle with a quantity of hosepipe. The first workboat would arrive at our setoff with an officer to climb aboard the

Lighthouse and help supervise the work alongside the three Keepers. The freshwater boat was first in line eager and ready to start.

The workboat came along side and watched for a period, just to see how much rise and fall there was and being satisfied, the heaving lines were passed across with the bow and stern ropes soon attached. The cox now signalled for the pump to begin after the hosepipe was passed to the keepers to put into the water tanks. Sometime later after, a grim-faced workman told the cox that the starting handle was missing and had been left aboard the ship, oh dear. After a lengthy period of shouting and shaking of fists, it was soon realised that there was no alternative but to return to the ship. Further shouting and bad language over the radio with the ship's Skipper brought the officer on our set off into the three-way communication. Pacing up and down showed a just held temper in check. The workboat it was decided had to return back to the ship for the missing handle. Cast of the restraining ropes, rewind the hosepipe and off they went fighting the choppy waves at breakneck speed. The officer was pacing up and down with a very red face and it was thought that perhaps it was best to say nothing.

The second workboat because of the space now vacated came alongside smartly complete with the heavy tanks of diesel. The ropes fore and aft were made fast and the hose for the diesel was passed across with the brass connection end to screw onto our very own screw connection, lo and behold yet another calamity, both hoses had female connections, what should of course be is a male hose end and a female hose end. The Lighthouse brass end was fixed, so the ship had got it wrong again. The radio was once more brought back into use and I didn't know what was said but the officer holding the radio well away from his ear didn't need much imagination to what was being said.

The disgruntled officer signalled to coil the hose back up and pass it back to the workboat and after casting off the ropes yet again, the workboat returned to the ship. Pulling the heavy water sodden ropes back onto the set off each time was heavy going and yet nothing so far had been landed. The tide and time was marching on and with the nearest rocks now beginning to break surface, speed was all important if stores were to be landed.

The now vacant space left by the diesel boat was once more filled by the water boat, practise makes perfect but with the tide getting lower and lower, the ropes were taking a lot more strain. The missing handle now held aloft was greeted with a loud cheer and the hose was passed and put into the water tank. "Can we please now get started?" the officer asked and the cox gave the signal to start pumping. The burly sour faced workman swung the engine time after time but perhaps, it should have been tested whilst aboard the ship. A second seaman pushed the first man out of the way and vented his full muscle to the task, but unfortunately, it failed to start. A foolish keeper at this point asked perhaps if it was out of diesel, the look was enough from the workboats crew to turn him into stone, so perhaps nothing else better be said. The pump is duff and dipping buckets into the tanks was also stated as an opinion but the humour was lost amongst the angry crewmen and the still pacing officer was spitting feathers. *Oh dear, back to the ship once again.* The three-way radio conversation was now at fervour pitch.

Now it was the turn once again for the diesel workboat, ropes were made fast the hose was passed across apparently with the right coupling, let's hope and pray this pump will fare better. The signal to start was given and the burly seaman put all his weight into swinging the handle, the engine caught first time and the fuel was pumping into the tanks. A pity the hose had numerous leaks along its joints but tight rags tied around the leaks soon stemmed the spills. The sea was getting a bit sloppy and the wind did seem to be gaining strength; this brought a shout for a new bow rope as the weight and strain had snapped the one in place. "Stop pumping!" shouted the cox, whilst another head rope was found. A temporary halt to the pumping whilst manoeuvring the boat back along-side; this meant that the hose also had to be uncoupled. The new bow rope was secured and the hose was once more back in place before pumping could commence again. The swell was getting uncomfortable but why the frustrated officer decided to kick the broken rope into the sea only he could say, but it drifted away and was soon forgotten.

Near finished with the first boatload of diesel and only another two boatloads before the tanks are finally full. Let's just hope no more calamitous things go wrong. When the tanks were empty, the ropes were cast off and the workboat returned to the ship for the next load.

The water boat was soon back in place and after tying up, the signal to start pumping water was given. Fresh water surged into the near empty tanks, another bow rope parted and a replacement had to be found and secured to further add to the officers rising anger. The radio was urging quicker turnarounds by the boats but nothing further could be done to speed things up. The Keepers could see that not much more could be done today as the tide was falling fast and only one more bowline was left. When the pump was finished and the boats tanks were empty, it was cast off for another load. It sped off at a rate of knots towards the ship but suddenly, a terrible noise was heard as the forgotten bow rope had somehow wrapped around the workboats prop. No power meant that the boat was wallowing in the waves and would soon be in trouble and be swamped without assistance. The full diesel boat went to her aid and a tow was soon fastened and the workboats made heavy work of going to back the ship.

The commander on the ship had seen enough and no more could be done, two boatloads only delivered and the frustrated officer was still getting earache on the radio. He was told to remain on the Lighthouse as the ship hoped to return tomorrow to finish landing operations. The language over the air waves were not for the faint hearted and a night on the Needles Lighthouse was not what the officer fancied but he unfortunately had no option, especially as he would now miss his dining aboard the 'Patricia' in the officer's mess. I did say that he could share my sausages for his tea. I think it was more of a grimace of acceptance than a thank you. The top bunk was free but he had no change of clothes. My shirt and trousers hung on him but they were clean and dry, pity he was a bit of a short, weedy fellow. Fog was forecast and we decided not to impart these glad tidings, as the fog signal would be the final straw for the poor fellow. Mind if there was fog, then the ship couldn't work the station but the officer would just have to lump it like the keepers.

The general feeling between the keepers was hopefully the fog will last and keep the ship away as going through all that nonsense again in trying to land stores would be avoided but realistically, it had to happen soon as fuel was still dangerously low. New bow ropes to make and hopefully the officer can be got ashore. Roll on relief day I might just be ashore myself before the ship returns and the opposite crew can do the business of landing the stores. My ever-depleting cupboard of food will not last long if the officer stays aboard the lighthouse for long.

Trinity House Puzzle

S	L	L	A	f	F	e	R	w	s	b	b
T	M	U	L	F	M	l	o	h	k	o	k
A	E	A	N	v	I	l	p	o	i	n	t
r	B	C	L	u	F	k	h	k	i	n	t
T	C	O	A	l	D	e	r	n	e	y	i
P	A	E	U	r	S	l	o	n	g	s	t
O	S	D	N	u	O	r	g	h	s	l	e
I	Q	D	Q	U	U	g	k	o	y	a	r
N	U	Y	U	i	T	i	c	n	a	b	n
T	E	S	S	a	H	t	a	r	c	a	l
T	T	T	S	i	B	s	b	a	o	e	b
G	O	O	D	w	I	n	s	o	u	t	h
T	r	N	A	i	S	s	e	a	n	n	e
S	O	E	E	t	H	a	p	p	i	s	b
P	P	S	H	f	O	e	s	s	t	r	u
R	M	A	R	y	P	o	r	t	r	e	v
A	G	E	R	s	P	t	n	i	o	p	e
W	C	O	Q	u	E	t	f	f	l	l	o
E	S	T	A	n	T	h	o	n	y	e	n
N	G	I	E	r	E	v	o	s	l	a	y

i	s	h	o	p	r	o	c	k	o	h	k
s	h	i	p	w	a	S	h	n	w	c	n
y	b	o	o	r	d	R	a	b	e	i	u
o	i	k	c	a	g	b	n	f	r	w	s
n	i	n	r	e	e	d	n	g	s	n	t
o	n	e	s	a	n	a	e	a	s	e	s
w	d	n	a	h	s	I	l	g	n	e	r
m	o	u	t	h	i	a	t	e	r	r	u
p	r	o	a	d	O	w	s	i	n	g	h
d	y	s	s	e	n	e	g	n	u	d	w
p	e	l	i	z	a	R	d	o	u	t	h
u	p	t	v	i	h	e	e	a	d	s	i
n	o	r	t	h	l	u	n	d	y	k	t
u	r	g	h	e	s	I	h	p	b	c	b
m	b	l	e	h	e	a	d	s	e	a	y
o	s	e	h	e	a	d	v	a	r	n	e
e	l	n	e	p	i	v	v	d	a	n	e
n	k	s	h	t	i	m	s	o	b	s	n
n	e	b	a	t	P	e	n	d	e	e	n
o	r	h	o	l	y	h	e	a	d	d	y

The list of Lighthouses and lightships that can be found in the grid, but one is missing from the list, can you spot which one that is?

49 Stations.

Greenwich. Bardsey. Shipwash. Strumble Head. Eddystone. Falls. Coquet. Mary Port. Lizard. Dungeness. Newarp. Nash. Dowsing. Whitby. Sandette. Goodwin South. Alderney. Start point. Longships. Sunk. Hanois. Owers. South Bishop. Happisburgh. Skokholm. Penlee point. Point Lynas. Caldy. Bar. Bishop Rock. Casquet. Varne. Smiths Knoll. English and welsh grounds. Trevose head. Royal Sovereign. North Lundy. Yarmouth. Pendeen. Wolf. Channel. Sark. Smalls. Longstone. Anvil point. Nab. Hurst. Hollyhead.

There are no prizes for getting the correct one that is missing, but it should get the old brain working.

Lightship or lighthouse? Go on give it a go, you can do it.

Trinity House

The lighthouse service has now to keep struggling on,
The lights do seem dimmer now the keepers are gone,
Fog signals are not wanted and nor are rock lights,
It's now a different service, it's totally lowered its sights.

'Twas always a pleasure to watch ships pass in the night,
The strength of the light beam, it was a wonderful sight,
Ships so they do tell us don't need keepers no more,
I suppose it's the way forward, but I can't be so sure.

You sure do get what you pay for or so they do say,
A second-class service, lights have had their day,
Computers and technology have now taken control,
I suppose it's the way forward, but it sure got no soul.

Well me old beauties, it's now redundancy for me,
The prospects are not rosy; I'll think you'll agree,
Cost cutters have done it, they have pruned to the bone,
I only hope that the shipping can get safely to home.

I've gone now, chucked out and finely been cast aside,
I don't mind really, I suppose what hurts is me pride,
Life is a bugger; it jumps up and kicks in your teeth,
The keepers will just have to look on in total disbelief.

I do wish that Trinity hadn't pushed ahead quite so fast,
Then the job could have been made the better to last,
A new way of life is needed, that's something that's so clear,
I'll just count me money and content myself with another
beer.

Troublesome Door

The fog signal at Nash Point Lighthouse is what is known as a 'siren', it's a real beauty. Twin horns sited from a turret pointing one up the Bristol Channel and the other pointed down. The engine room with the fog signal perched on its roof dominates the clifftop between the two lighthouse towers. One tower to the east and one tower to the west. The western tower with two adjacent dwellings is no longer used as a lighthouse but the eastern tower has all the modern equipment in present day technology to enable a constant flashing light warning to shipping.

The engine room and fog signal for obvious reasons is sited well away from the dwellings roughly halfway between both. But even with double glazing, the sequenced two second blast every 45 seconds; it still shakes the window frames. The engine room houses the two giant diesel compressors and the standby generator together with the air receiver tanks.

Thursday morning watch routine says that everything should be checked and made in good order.

The fog signal is given a run and both coders are tested. The mains electricity is failed to make sure the standby generator kicks into life. The Principal Keeper, this particular morning watch, was on duty and decided to look into the pump room which is accessed through a separate outside door from the engine room. Today, unfortunately, it was well and truly stuck fast. The painters, having just completed their work on station, had slapped an extra two coats of paint on the door and what with wet winter weather conditions a swelling of the door frame meant that the tight-fitting door just wouldn't budge.

It should be stated here perhaps that the Principal Keeper, although a likable fellow, was tenacious in getting the job done, anything was achievable, he often quoted and his years of experience told him to find a way. To complete the testing was a priority. I did think that kicking the door with his size ten steel toecap boots was perhaps a little foolhardy and of course it didn't make any impression on the door except to take off a great deal of the paintwork and his new work boots showed a nasty tear in the leather covering. "We will soon see who is boss here," he shouted, and stomped off to the work-shed. He returned with a long-handled sledgehammer and said to stand clear as a few taps with this fearsome weapon would soon cure the problem. After several hefty blows, the stubborn door finally yielded and fell open with a crash.

I did notice that perhaps the paint would have to be touched up, as now several large patches seemed to have appeared. The pumping apparatus was soon checked and the fuel header tanks showed everything in good order. The door now had to be closed again and after a few tentative bangs to close, it was shown that perhaps more robust action was required to close the door, oh dear. John, the Principal Keeper, was hopping up and down with his hand in his mouth trying to stem his bloodied hand after being overzealous with the pulling, cursing and shouting through the undoubted pain I thought was understandable. The door handle perhaps should have been better positioned it just might have saved his now bleeding knuckles. When John had calmed down and dressed his wounds, a full stock of the situation was assessed and a new plan of attack was worked out. What was required was a heavy rope. The rope locker was in the shed along with all the station tools and of course, the key was on the bunch now wedged between door and door-jam.

Nothing else for it but back to the sledge hammer again. Several more blows upon the troublesome door soon had it sprung open again and the paintwork was showing further damage. The keys on inspection were in a very poor state, one was twisted completely in half one was bent almost double and a yale key was now in two pieces. The vice in the engine room soon had the twisted key back straight again but the bent key broke in half. The good key, luckily, was the one that fitted this troublesome door. The rope was fetched and one end was attached to the door handle. After checking that everything was ready, no keys in the lock, and stand back, the Principal Keeper gave a hefty pull on the rope and the door crashed into the doorframe. However, the handle was ripped off and now dangled on the end of the rope. The sledgehammer had ended up in the small of John's back as he fell over in pulling the rope so hard and it was then tossed at the metal water gratings, it bounced on its handle and disappeared over the cliff to the beach some 60ft below. A long trek will have to be made to retrieve the hammer, as access to the beach is way along the cliff top, I just hope nobody was anywhere near when it dropped.

John's shout of triumph, that's cured that he said, but what was soon apparent was that the mortise lock was way out of alignment and even with the good key, it will need the attention of a good carpenter.

The rope was coiled up to return to the tool shed and it of course was locked (security mad) the broken key was no good now as it was in two pieces. An angry yell and the window next to the doorframe was the next to feel the full fury of John's feelings, the other keeper and myself decided to stay silent and say nothing. No telling whom next might get a load of verbal through frustration on John's part. The screwdriver and some much larger screws soon had the handle securely replaced but the door was stuck fast now and the handle was only decoration. The blood saturated cloth bandage did strike a further reminder that the handle would be better placed away from the doorframe, but that will be for another day.

The painting over of the tell-tale signs could wait. New keys would have to be found for the tool shed and the troublesome door. A new piece of glass to replace the broken window could be purchased along with some putty. The afternoon Keeper, perhaps, could stroll down the beach to retrieve the sledgehammer, I just hoped the tide was out.

John, bless him, did see the funny side over a cup of tea, but expenditure for glass, keys, paint and putty would have to be explained, I expect all will put right. "Please also send a works carpenter as a troublesome door needs attention," he said.

Virtuous Keeper

I don't know why but I am described by my fellow lighthouse keepers as a jolly good egg and as an exemplary work colleague. A pleasure to share the cooped up cramped conditions whilst on board the Lighthouse. I very seldom use bad language, I don't now smoke, drinking is taboo, loose women are never of any interest and I am early to bed and early to rise. What a boring fellow you are I hear you say. My work is diligent and I do try and exercise regularly, but forever going around in circles every day on this tower rock do make things very difficult. I don't get any reward or praise for all this self-denial, but obviously the lack of spending on such necessities like cigarettes, beer and loose women do save me a considerable sum of money. But do look out all this will change when I'm finally put ashore from the confines of my tower lighthouse prison.

Cigarettes Puzzle

A poor old lighthouse keeper was down on his luck and unable to afford the luxury of cigarettes but he did so like a good old smoke, so he collected dog ends. He was once a man of means but since his forced redundancy and money was tight, it was give up smoking entirely to make ends meet. What a shame, but a solution to this problem was in collecting other people's cast offs. He found that shredding the tobacco and putting it in a tin until he had enough to make a roll up cigarette usually took about seven butt ends. By emptying the tobacco from the cork tip, he was also ensured the new fag would be free from other people's mouth saliva or lipstick.

Seven fag ends rolled into a new cigarette, he could continue to enjoy his smoking habit without it costing any money except the purchase of fag papers. *Good reasoning*, he thought.

The first day on working out this solution to his problem, he found four cigarette ends in the gutter and an additional eight in an ashtray, three more in an old paint tin and five more in the lobby of the local hotel. He did get some funny looks from different people but what the heck, at least he could have a smoke.

He scraped together enough for a half pint in the local pub where he managed to collect another 15 fag ends. He discovered four more in the rubbish bin and six more on the way home. Getting home the Trinity House jacket pocket produced four more fag butts in the pockets.

He was in clover and soon had enough cigarettes rolled up to smoke himself to death.

How many cigarettes could he have produced altogether from his collection of fag ends.

Golf Club Committee Dilemma

The Golf Committee met to sort out a complaint from myself about the cheating of a member whilst playing a cup game round on the links course. My playing partner opponent had hit the ball into thick rough vegetation. After searching for a considerable time, I managed to put my big feet right on top of the lost ball. The ball was quickly transferred to my pocket without my opponent seeing. A few moments later, I hear a loud shout from the undergrowth saying, "Ah, hear it is." *Well, the little liar,* I thought, I am not very pleased and reported the incident to the club captain.

What do you think happened at the committee meeting? Things didn't work out as I expected.

Where's Me Chop

The morning watchman starting his period of duty at 0400 which would last until 1200. He was responsible for being cook of the day amongst his other duties. The checking of the engines and making out the light before hanging up the curtains was just part of the varied list of jobs. Cleaning and washing down the tower whilst the other two keepers were in bed was soon completed so that the Rayburn coke scuttle could be filled in readiness for the cooking of the daily lunch. Plenty of heat in the oven to make sure there would be no problems about the 1300 normal time serving. All three keepers usually sat down together at this time to enjoy the meal. Most keepers are very good cooks and after years of practise their culinary skills know no bounds. The smell of fresh bread was often wafting up to the bedroom level making getting up for breakfast a pleasure.

The usual serving of meat and vegetables is down to what each keeper has put out for cooking. Cook of the day supplies the vegetables and the meat or pie is down to what you want. Roast potatoes are nearly always on the menu and go well with most things.

On my arrival into the kitchen after my middle watch for breakfast, I was told that I had better get something out for my dinner as I had obviously forgotten. "That can't be right," I said, as I had put out a nice pork chop.

"Well, where is it then," the cook asked. "I can't cook what isn't here." In total disbelief, I had to get another out of the freezer, something's not right here, as I was sure I had left it on the window recess as normal. Nothing further was said and the meal was completed in a satisfactory manner.

Perhaps I was dreaming or losing my marbles. Something strange is going on here.

Two days later whilst on the same watch routine, I was greeted in exactly the same manner at breakfast time with the cook asking what I wanted for my dinner as yet again, I hadn't put out anything for him to cook. I looked at him dumbfounded and thought he was having a laugh but he was adamant that nothing was left out. "What happened to my sausages?" I asked.

"I haven't seen any sausages." I reluctantly made a visit once again to the freezer for more sausages, otherwise no dinner for me. I did think that the two keepers were having a joke and playing silly blighters, and at this rate, my supply of food would not last the month.

Next morning, it was my turn to be cook of the day. I had just returned from the engine room back into the kitchen, when a saw a big, black back seagull on the window sill with the Keeper's offerings to be cooked in his beak, sausages and a pie by the looks of it. The penny dropped, that's where my chop and sausages had gone, the naughty blighter, and throwing a tea towel at him made him scarper quickly, what a sneak thief. The gull flew off smacking his beak and obviously had been waiting his chance, he was on a good thing. When the keepers arrived for breakfast, I told them the story about the opportunist gull and asked perhaps if they could get me something to cook or else they would get no dinner. Needless to say, there after any meat for dinner was left well out of reach of thieving seagulls and calm was once more restored. At the time, I did wonder who was mucking about, but seemingly, I was misinformed. And apologies all around were accepted.